Death on Torrid Avenue

Also by Patricia McLinn

Secret Sleuth series

Death on the Diversion

Death on Torrid Avenue

Death on Beguiling Way

Death on Covert Circle

Death on Shady Bridge

Death on Carrion Lane

Death on ZigZag Trail

Death on Puzzle Place

Caught Dead in Wyoming series

Sign Off

Left Hanging

Shoot First

Last Ditch

Look Live

Back Story

Cold Open

Hot Roll

Reaction Shot

Body Brace

Cross Talk

Air Ready

Holiday Bullets

Cue Up

The Innocence Series

Proof of Innocence

Price of Innocence

Premise of Innocence

Death on Torrid Avenue

Secret Sleuth, Book 2

Patricia McLinn

PROLOGUE

YOU DON'T KNOW about me without you have read a book by the name of *Death on the Diversion*. It told the truth, mainly...

And you don't remember the opening of *The Adventures of Huckleberry Finn* by Mark Twain if you're about to correct my grammar.

No worries if you don't know about me. I'll fill you in on Sheila Mackey as we go along.

If you don't remember or have never read *Huck Finn*, give it a try.

I was in my new-to-me house, staring at the spine of my copy of Huck Finn, squished into a bookshelf mostly taken over by mysteries in the small office, and thinking about lies, secrets, and various facets of telling or not telling the truth.

Unlike Huck's adventures along the Mississippi River, mine started with a leap from Manhattan to North Bend County, Kentucky.

Also unlike the peripatetic Huck, I intended to stay put.

Especially on this blustery mid-February day that raised my appreciation for central heat, electric lights, and microwaves to rescue tea rapidly approaching tepid.

Gracie had other ideas.

Gracie is a dog.

Specifically, she's a rough collie. Think *Lassie*.

I adopted Gracie through collie rescue a month ago and shortly after moving into this house. I was getting to know house and dog simultaneously.

The house was about seventy years old. The dog was less than one.

Both were part of my grand plan for my future. The grand plan had left what kind of house open to whatever struck me. Which turned out to be a somewhat worn but sturdy post-World War II red brick colonial.

My dog choice had a few prerequisites: Big and furry, good to hug.

Gracie was big and furry. She wasn't wild about hugs, but she'd stand or lie still for petting if she didn't have better things to do.

Right now she thought she had far, far better things to do.

Gracie's ears heralded her approach.

They appeared just over the edge of the desk. All I could see were those two ears—with their tips dropped down in unequal folds, her left ear tending to stand more upright than the right—proceeding along the edge of the old desk.

She cleared the desk corner and presented herself at the side of my chair, where I'd been contemplating truth, lies, secrets, and Huck Finn while unpacking files into drawers in the bedroom designated as my office.

What I'd *do* in that office remained a mystery.

My grand plan had a blank or two.

Gracie stared at me with intent and intelligent brown eyes.

With her built-in fur coat, I doubted she concerned herself much about central heat, hot tea, or blustery February days.

According to Gracie's clock, it was time to go to the dog park. Gracie's clock ran fast when it came to meals, treats, and the dog park.

I sighed.

I also picked up my phone and called an acquaintance I'd met on my first trip to the dog park a month ago. Clara Woodrow owned LuLu, a dog Gracie had instantly become attached to.

Yes, I was making a play date for my dog.

You might be thinking I had nothing to complain about with Gracie's clock moving up, since sitting in my unpurposed office thinking about Huckleberry Finn, lies, truth, and secrets while unloading files did not constitute a jam-packed day.

On the other hand, it was not a sultry summer day on the Mississippi, but a sleet-spitting monochrome morning near the Ohio River, which is where North Bend County, Kentucky sits.

"I know we'd be the only ones out there on a day like this—" I said to Clara, giving her an easy out, since no sane person would say yes to a dog play date in this weather. "—but would you consider meeting us at the dog park?"

Clara and LuLu—asked the question "Want to see Gracie?"—said yes.

"Don't worry, we won't be alone," Clara said.

Things might have turned out differently if we had been.

CHAPTER ONE

THE TORRID AVENUE Dog Park is a meritocracy. You are not judged by what you wear, how much money you have, or what you do for a living.

Not even, entirely, on how well behaved your dog is. And certainly not by what your dog looks like.

You are judged on how you treat your dog and whether you pick up poop.

Official signs instruct owners to pick up after their dogs, but that pales compared to the peer pressure.

Among the regular dog park denizens, those who pay it forward by picking up extra poop beyond their own dog's are the top echelon. Those scofflaws who leave their dog's poop for the good citizens to pick up are the dregs. In between comes a wide swath of live-and-let-livers.

At least that's how it sorts out for most of the easygoing visitors to the Torrid Avenue Dog Park.

However, there is a small and strident subculture of vehements who divide into two warring factions having nothing to do with picking up poop: the Dwights and the Bobs.

The bad news from my point of view as Gracie and I arrived at the park Wednesday, was two of the five vehicles already there belonged to the leaders of those factions. Dwight Yagos and Bob Coble.

Judging by the generous clusters of Boston terrier bumper stickers and decals, a third vehicle belonged to Berrie Vittlow, who always brought a swarm of Boston terriers. It was impossible—at least for me—to tell if she brought the same dogs every time or a rotating crop. For a reason that will soon become apparent, we've never had enough conversation for me to clarify whether all the Bostons were hers or if she ran a breed-specific day care.

Since Gracie and LuLu qualified as large dogs, our dog park worlds offered minimal direct overlap with Berrie's small dogs, but sound carries. And Berrie was a vocal member of the Bob Coble camp. Very vocal. Some of her Bostons were also vocal, especially Marcus.

The fourth vehicle belonged to an older man named Ronald, who volunteered at the shelter, conveniently located across Torrid Avenue, and frequently brought shelter dogs for exercise and—depending on the personality of the shelter dog—for socializing.

I didn't recognize the final vehicle. A sturdy four-wheel drive with no decals or bumper stickers, but new Kentucky plates. I recognized their newness, because my plates had a similar gloss under the road spray.

Berrie—what better name for a Boston terrier devotee?—would be in the small-dog enclosure with the Bostons. Even if Ronald and the stranger had large dogs, that likely wasn't enough population to keep Dwight and Bob adequately separated.

Darn.

Clara and I might be pressed into service as buffers.

Spotting her vehicle pulling in, I buttoned, zipped, snapped, and tightened the layers I'd loosened in the relative warmth of my car.

"I'm telling you, the Dwights and Bobs are getting out of hand," Clara said as soon as she emerged from her substantial SUV, making it clear she'd made the same assessments I had.

We waited—me more patiently than Gracie—while Clara, still talking, unloaded long-legged LuLu, whose parentage might include Great Pyrenees, greyhound, some sort of setter, or anything else making her long, tall, thin, and a true character.

"Something's going to happen. I mean *really* happen."

Clara's foreboding was muffled, since I had the hood of my parka pulled up. "Like what?"

"Like … like a fight—a real fight! Or worse," she said ominously.

"I think we should ban Dwight and Bob. Get up a petition, have everybody sign, take it to the park district, and say we don't want either of them here."

Neither Dwight nor Bob would strike you as a dangerous person if you passed him on the street.

On the other hand, they're probably fine on the street. It's the dog park and each other that bring out their worst.

Neither is an official dog trainer. That doesn't stop them from having opinions. Many, many opinions. They extol somewhat different methods. It's not that one beats dogs and the other only praises. It's more subtle. In fact, most times I can't tell a difference.

But the vehements can and do.

Perhaps I'd have thought my short tenure as a dog owner explained why I couldn't tell a difference. Except there's a third group at the dog park. The Sane Middles, as Donna describes us.

No one disputed Donna's role as the quasi-official Torrid Avenue Dog Park no-nonsense mother figure. She was a veteran dog-owner, friendly, and blunt.

Passing her inquisition the first day I brought Gracie here had been a milestone in the acceptance of my cover story. Why a cover story? That goes back to secrets, truth, and lies. We'll get there.

For now, the focus is on the feuding parties at the dog park.

"You think the Dwights and Bobs would sign a petition to ban their leaders?" I asked Clara. "The other guy, sure, but not their own."

She waved that off, and lost LuLu's leash.

But with Gracie still leashed, LuLu wasn't going anywhere, giving Clara a chance to reclaim putative control of her dog.

As we walked past the enclosure closest to the parking lot, which was also the smaller of the large-dog areas, Ronald came to the fence line to say hello.

The Torrid Avenue Dog Park is shaped like a lumpy pie with a squat wedge cut out. That wedge accommodated access from the parking lot, a PortaPotty, trash bins, and a water spout. The four dog enclosures—two for small dogs, two for large dogs—met at the narrow part of the wedge in a sort of vestibule area. Once inside the vestibule's main gate, you could choose to enter any enclosure by way of an individual gate. A rectangle of concrete sat inside each enclosure's gate. Beyond came patchy grass and, in this weather, mud.

"Got a young one today," Ronald said, bypassing any chit-chat about mere humans and getting to the vital topic of dogs. "Not sure yet I can trust him with LuLu or Gracie." He left a mini-beat of silence. "Or any other dogs around."

Clara and I nodded solemnly, knowing full well he could have the mildest dog in the history of four paws with him and he still would avoid the other large dog area, because that's where Bob and Dwight were.

Bob with Trevalyn, a Gordon setter registered with the American Kennel Club.

Dwight with Skeeter, a black mouth cur mix.

No slight intended with "cur"—that's the breed's name. Though Dwight said Skeeter had other breeds thrown in.

Now, observing the mostly black shelter dog stretched out on the cold ground happily chewing on a toy, it occurred to me Ronald might actually *have* the mildest dog in the history of four paws with him.

But by using this shelter dog as his excuse to escape Dwight and Bob, Ronald blocked us from joining him. Or admit we preferred exposing our dogs to an animal he'd warned us off to sharing an enclosure with Bob and Dwight.

After a few comments on the dogs (good) and the weather (lousy), he ambled off and we continued toward the vestibule's entry.

"See," Clara said. "Something needs to be done. When they're scaring off a sweet guy like Ronald … As for the Dwights and Bobs not signing the petition, we don't even ask them. We go for the normal people. Like you and me."

"I'm touched." She doesn't know my history, or she might reconsider.

All she knew was I'd arrived in North Bend County without a job or family bringing me here, which was unheard of, and I had adopted a rescue dog.

I suspected that for Clara only the last fact counted.

I stopped Gracie outside the main gate, taking the opportunity to command a "sit" when she craved freedom.

She dropped her wiggling bottom toward the ground. I pretended not to notice it never made contact before she sprang up.

Our target enclosure stretched from its tip at the vestibule to outer fences forming part of the misshapen edge of that lumpy pie. The ground was mostly flat, but with a dip in what would be right field in baseball. Just beyond the fence a stand of trees partially masked a creek.

That dip inside the fence, the only spot where the dogs were out of sight, was nicknamed Las Vegas—it was a gamble letting your dog go there and even good dogs could go rogue in the riotous atmosphere of no oversight.

Dog park humor.

Past the creek and a large stand of trees sat the county sheriff's department and jail in a relatively recent building, certainly less than two decades. Compared to much of Haines Tavern, Kentucky, the North Bend County seat, that made it brand spanking new.

"Oh, look," Clara said in a conspiratorial whisper, masked from Berrie's listening ears by the predicable squeak of the main gate. Berrie frequently stayed near the vestibule, allowing her to critique owners entering any enclosure. "It's the new dog with the new guy."

"What new dog with what new guy?"

I wasn't in a position to look because Gracie, in her eagerness to get to the wide-open spaces of the enclosure, was braiding her leash and my legs.

"Gracie, sit."

I got out the command as two sounds reached us.

The louder was the barking of Marcus the Boston terrier, soon backed by his brethren in the small-dog enclosure.

The Bostons, including the females, reminded me of William Powell in the *Thin Man* movies. None more so than Marcus, their obvious leader. The tuxedo styling of his black and white coat, the wide-set and slightly pouchy eyes, the jowly lower face.

But Powell's Nick Charles never lost his cool the way Marcus did under one particular stimulus.

Me.

I had no idea why. Nobody did. I never harmed or teased or treated or even acknowledged the dog. First time he saw me, he went berserk. And every time since.

From the far side of the small-dog enclosure, he raced toward the vestibule, emitting the gruff bark of his breed, as if they're rolling r's with abandon.

Reaching the gate, he jumped straight up. It felt like he'd reach my eye level any second. In between spates of jumping, he ran in crazy circles, fancied up with shoulder rolls and spins. All the while barking.

He didn't sound vicious, just insane.

Barely audible over Marcus came the already all-too-familiar human voice. "Don't let her wrap around you like that. It's what Bob says—"

Clara and I exchanged eye-rolls.

But then I had to refocus on Gracie. Not only because I'd told her to sit and it's vital to follow through on a command—otherwise you train your dog to ignore you, according to ninety-two percent of the eighty-seven dog training books I've read, not to mention dozens of videos watched, plus the class we're attending at the local pet store— but also because she'd started a boa constrictor number on my legs.

I clicked my tongue. Maybe that caught Gracie's attention. Or my earlier words percolated through her excitement to her listening center. Or she ran out of leash and was as stuck as I was. Whatever the cause, Gracie sat and looked up at me.

"Good girl." With one hand, I started her back the opposite direction. She made it around several times, but each revolution seemed to stretch her patience more. At the end, I pivoted to speed the process.

"If you'd listened to what Bob told you the first time you came here, you'd have much better control of your dog. He's so generous with his knowledge and expertise. You shouldn't—"

I ignored Berrie by bending to unhook the leash from Gracie's collar.

"Ready?" Clara asked. She already had LuLu unhooked. LuLu had completed two training courses and although she danced a bit, she held her position. Clara's hand was on the gate's latch.

"Gracie, wait," I ordered.

Clara opened the gate. We silently counted together. Right at *three,* and a millisecond before Gracie bolted, we both said, "Okay."

The dogs sprang forward, leaping and twisting. Gracie emitted one ecstatic bark, and they were off at full speed.

"See you later, Berrie!" I called, as if she'd only said hello.

Still under the cover of Marcus' noise, Clara returned to her earlier subject. "What new dog is a lab mix named Murphy loping over to meet our girls. And the new guy is the one who's by our table." Each enclosure held two or three roof-covered picnic tables and we favored the one farthest from the enclosure Berrie was in.

But I didn't look at the table. I searched Bob's and Dwight's locations.

Bob—in his knee-high boots, tweed cap, and jacket with dark fabric across the shoulders suitable for shooting in the English countryside—was to our far left, along the fence to the other small-dog enclosure, which was empty. Dwight—with his University of Kentucky baseball cap under the hood of an aged UK blue jacket, and ever-present blue and white hand-knit scarf with foot-long fringe—was almost as far to our right, standing on the slight rise looking down into the out-of-sight Las Vegas dip.

Good news. We wouldn't be called on for peacekeeping.

I took two steps across the concrete pad inside the enclosure. Marcus turned off like I hit the power button on his remote.

Dropping her voice as we stepped off the concrete into mud generally too churned by dog feet to freeze, Clara continued, "They were here yesterday. I met them then. Murphy's a lab, maybe a lab mix. See? Over there. Green coat."

To my relief, Clara meant the guy, not the dog, wore a green coat.

The dog was golden colored except for splashes of white on its toes.

The guy wasn't by our table, he was sitting on it. That didn't bother me any. Not only was February not the time to think about eating off its surface, but we mostly sat on the top, too, because as I'd seen when a brief warm spell brought out more dogs, the table's lower regions were a favorite peeing target for males. Canines, that is.

"He's just moved to the area." Clara talked fast, getting in her information before even our lackadaisical pace brought us within the guy's hearing. "Donna talked to him and said he has some experience with dogs and common sense. His lab mix is a sweetheart. She also said the guy's quite nice."

"Lab mix? Not all lab?" I asked.

"I didn't ask specifically," Clara said. "But he's tall and long for lab. Plus the white on the toes probably indicates not a purebred, don't you think?"

My knowledge of Labrador retriever DNA and breed confirmation logged in at barely above zero.

"Berrie said she encountered Murphy with the Bostons in the entry the day before yesterday and he was well behaved."

I suspected that was more than could be said for the Bostons. They were friendly to humans—with the Marcus-and-me exception— but renowned at the dog park for bullying other dogs. In particular, mild-mannered bigger dogs. Not-so-mild-mannered bigger dogs they left alone.

They're not stupid.

As much as Berrie critiqued other owners' techniques, she apparently saw nothing worth commenting about in *her* dogs' behavior.

That left the possibility that Berrie's impression of good behavior on the part of this lab mix might have been abject terror.

"Oh, look," Clara said again. "LuLu and Gracie seem to be getting along with the new dog."

After the *Hi, how are you* interlude, including the requisite close and personal smelling, Gracie had bounced away, looking back over her shoulder, inviting the newcomer to her favorite game.

This could test the lab mix's amiability. Gracie did her best to live up to her heritage as a herding dog by chasing her dog park buddies and herding them to whichever corner struck her fancy. With LuLu, she added a bit of mild neck chewing if she didn't obey fast enough.

Yes, my dog was bossy.

But in a cute way. Really.

Not at all like the Bostons. That's not bias. Other owners had said so.

As Donna said, Gracie waited until she was friends with a dog before bossing it around, which made it play. "Except for the German shepherd who keeps trying to mount her and she keeps telling him to knock it off—*that* she means," Donna told me. "He just hasn't caught on yet."

Clara was kind enough to refer to Gracie as the park's referee. And it's true she would get between scuffling dogs, barking in reprimand, and generally trying to bring order.

In public I went along with Clara's description of her as the referee.

Privately, I chided Gracie. *When a female is already a bitch by definition, it doesn't hurt to add a little kindness,* I informed her. It might not be fair, but it's true.

Listening to myself, I felt like I'd channeled my great-aunt Kit, with whom I'd shared a Manhattan brownstone and a secret life for the past decade and a half. Though Kit wouldn't have waited for private to make her pronouncement.

The other dogs did not seem to mind Gracie's bossiness, not even the German shepherd who still hadn't accepted Gracie's *Not Interested.*

Perhaps the other dogs accepted Gracie's bossiness because she never competed for the various balls thrown around. Retrievers chased balls, Gracie chased retrievers. Seemed to work for everyone.

Clara and I halted some distance from the table to watch the dogs.

I pulled my right hand free of its glove-then-mitten covering to tighten the drawstring on my parka hood, which came loose during Gracie's ring-around-the-owner exercise. My eyebrows had started to freeze.

"Your nails look wonderful," Clara said.

I looked around, then saw her looking at my hand. I followed her gaze and experienced a spurt of surprise.

I'd forgotten.

I have strong nails that get too long to be neat without manicures. Until becoming the public face for *Abandon All*, I hadn't been able to afford manicures. After, my duties kept me busy enough that I rarely took the time.

Yes, there it is.

My big secret.

I was the person the world knew as the author of *Abandon All*, the biggest blockbuster novel and movie of the past couple decades. Under a different name. And under false pretenses, since my great-aunt Kit, a career novelist, actually wrote the book.

The masquerade was her idea.

So was her retirement and selling the Manhattan brownstone we'd shared this past fall. In other words, she started me on this new life.

One where I had time to contemplate Huck Finn, dog park mores, and secrets, truth, and lies. One where I also moved to Kentucky, bought my own house, adopted a rescue collie, and had a manicure.

A whole new world.

The hitch is that the now me not be outed as the *Abandon All* me. Or I'll have no chance to find out who the non-*Abandon All* me is.

"Thank you." I held up my hand to admire it. "I treated myself to a manicure. My nails are usually long and raggedy."

"Mine are never too long. Good for you for getting a manicure. I tried to, too, for a while. Ned urged me to include it in the monthly budget, that sweet man. But in the last year of my mother-in-law's illness and then with a new dog…"

As I nodded—acknowledgement both of how caring for her mother-in-law wouldn't have allowed time for manicures and how hard dogs were on manicures—I noted a bemused half grin on the new guy's face. He'd clearly been eavesdropping. Just as clearly, he didn't get manicures.

Not in either sense of *get*—having one himself or understanding the ins and outs of them. He appeared amused by his lack of comprehension.

"Hi, Teague," Clara called to him, raising a hand in greeting. "Looks like we might have a three-way bond forming here."

Our gazes met for an amiable instant, then naturally shifted to our dogs.

They made quite a trio. Gracie's coat, with variations of browns to golds, as well as white and touches of black, bridged LuLu's pale buff and his dog's deeper golden.

But that was temporary. They'd all be mud colored soon.

"What's your dog's name?" I asked as Clara and I sat on the tabletop, hip-length jackets tucked carefully under derrieres, feet on the bench.

"Murphy."

"Ah, a male."

"Neutered," Clara said immediately. "Stray. About two years old. He's had him about six months. His second rescue."

"Pretty much covers it. The collie's yours?" he asked me.

"Uh-huh. Gracie. Rescue. Best guess is under a year old. I've had her a month. First dog of my own." Answering the usual dog park questions all at once saved a lot of time.

Watching the dogs, I didn't see his expression, but heard his grin. "Now that the important stuff is covered, I'm Teague O'Donnell."

"Teague as in rhymes with League," Clara said.

"Teague O'Donnell," I repeated. "Italian, huh?"

He laughed, then tried to deadpan. "Pure Sicilian. You?"

"Oh my gosh." Clara clapped her thickly covered hands, creating a dull *whumph*. "I should have introduced you two. I'm so sorry."

"No worries, Clara. We'll go self-service," I said. He removed his glove and extended his hand to me. Without removing the coverings protecting my skin from frostbite, I met his grip. "Call me Sheila M."

"*Call* you Sheila M.?" His mouth quirked. He also held onto my hand. No way that made a physical impression through the mitten-covered gloves I wore, yet it had an impact. I'd have to make a big deal of it to withdraw my hand. I could—would—if necessary, but for the moment, I was suspended, judging the necessity. "Sounds like an alias, as if Sheila isn't your real name."

Clara laughed, "She always says that—Call me Sheila M." She laughed again. "Let me do this proper now. Sheila Mackey meet

Teague O'Donnell. That's his dog, Murphy. He's a substitute teacher and tutor for the high school."

I withdrew my hand.

Great.

A high school teacher.

I'd thought my cover story had been so brilliant. And here I was, barely a month into it, meeting somebody who actually did what I claimed to have retired from … from which I claimed to have retired.

To pass as an English teacher I'd have to watch my grammar. *Abandon All* used enough informal structures that I'd never worried about proper grammar in interviews, lectures, and appearances.

I mentally added this guy to a stay-away-from list that had been blessedly empty until now.

Unfortunately, staying away from him might be trickier than it sounded, since Gracie, LuLu, and Murphy were frolicking like they'd come from the same litter.

"Oh, aren't they cute," Clara cooed. "They'll never want to be separated."

CHAPTER TWO

"**CLARA TOLD ME** yesterday how she took care of her ill mother-in-law for so long and her husband's insisting she takes a good break and that's why she can be here with LuLu every day. What do you do, Sheila, that lets you bring Gracie to the dog park daily?" Teague asked.

What was with this guy and questions?

He'd already pelted me with several. Native or not? How long I'd lived here? What brought me here? House or apartment? And more. I'd answered a few, sidestepped most.

Before I could—or had to—answer this one, we heard raised voices from near the picnic table on the opposite side of our enclosure.

Turning toward the voices—Bob and Dwight—meant squinting into stinging sleet.

Darn. It was always easier to keep the peace if you kept the two of them separated. But we'd been distracted and Bob must have gotten past us. Because he was now over by Dwight.

In a loud, sneering tone, Bob Coble flung out a dismissive arm. "You have no control over that animal."

"They're getting worse, and worse." Clara tipped her head toward Dwight and Bob. If they'd been paying attention, they'd have known she was talking about them no matter how low her voice. As it was, they were too intent on arguing to catch head tips. "The dogs are picking up on the tension."

Since our three dogs trotted along the fence line, happily trying to get three big dog mouths on a five-inch stick, punctuated by dramatic sound effects, I assumed she meant Dwight's and Bob's dogs, not ours.

Skeeter and Trevalyn milled around their owners, looking up at the angry faces.

"Go to hell," Dwight snapped back.

"Look, look," Bob crowed triumphantly. "He broke hold. Right there. That's what I mean."

I expected Dwight to jump on the fact Bob's dog, Trevalyn, wasn't holding, either.

"You're an—" Dwight said a word I hadn't heard him or anyone else use at the Torrid Avenue Dog Park. I'd heard it frequently on TV and in Manhattan, including from tots at playgrounds, but it shocked me here.

Perhaps it shocked Dwight, too, because he turned, the fringe swinging on the scarf I'd never seen him without, and walked away from Bob.

That surprised me, too. These arguments usually ran a lot longer than this, touching on wide-ranging areas of dog grooming, feeding, naming, and more, in addition to training.

"Those two always like that?" Teague asked.

"Sometimes it's worse," Clara said. "If their various followers are around, they pile in, too. Plus, an audience gets those two more wound up. This was short."

Over the past weeks, I'd heard them argue about the ideal way to hook a leash, doggie seatbelts vs. other car restraints, whether saying "no" was an aversive, and more.

I couldn't take it too seriously. It was chest-puffing, steam letting-off, schoolyard antics for supposed grown-ups.

Though it certainly made the dog park more pleasant when they didn't interact. Better yet, when neither was here. I wondered if Clara's petition idea stood a chance.

Clara told Teague about last week, when she and I listened as a dust-up between Dwight and Bob over whether deli turkey or home-cooked chicken was the better treat.

Donna stopped the deli turkey-home-cooked chicken feud by whacking each of their puff-coated arms with a doubled over leash and telling them to knock it off.

Now, Clara said exactly what I was thinking. "Too bad Donna isn't here."

"She's one of the few who can cool their ardor," I added.

"Are you saying passions run high at Torrid Avenue Dog Park?" asked this new guy with an amused glint in his light green eyes. "Appropriate, considering the address."

"Exactly. Although the passions tend to focus on fur rather than romance," Clara said.

I followed with, "Making the passions even more *fervent*."

After we'd all chuckled, he said, "Before those two interrupted, you were telling me what you're doing at the dog park, Sheila."

"Freezing."

He gave a half-smile. Something about it left me unsettled. "I meant how can you be with Clara on weekdays. I come when there's no substituting job. Some folks work nights, some are retired. Clara is resting up after a long stint of caregiving. What about you?"

Before I could say anything to push back—politely, but definitively—against his nosy question, Clara said cheerfully, "Oh, Sheila's so fortunate. She came into an inheritance."

"Did she?" His tone added to my unsettled feeling.

It had no impact on Clara. "I mean, not fortunate, because to inherit, someone else has to die, but in this case it was quite a distant relative she hardly knew, but they were the only ones in the family named Sheila, and she'd lived a long time—the relative I mean—and the inheritance let Sheila quit her job and move here for a more relaxing life. Though with all the house projects she has going—"

"What kind of job did she quit?"

Was it my imagination or was this guy incredibly nosy? True, Clara only told him things I'd willingly told her at the start of our acquaintance, but she hadn't grilled me the way he was.

Plus, she'd accepted anything I'd said.

Either my imagination had jumped to paranoia or Teague O'Donnell was not totally accepting. Not into full-blown suspicion, but a pervasive film of skepticism.

Who *was* this guy?

"She taught English. High school English. Isn't that a coincidence, with you being a high school teacher, too?"

"It is," he said to Clara, but he looked at me.

"I did," I said cheerfully and with all the confidence and experience of presenting myself as the author of *Abandon All* for fifteen years.

"So, fur and fervent—English teacher humor?"

"Absolutely."

"Can you imagine inheriting enough money that you don't have to work anymore?" Clara sounded excited for me, with no tinge of envy. Impossible not to like her. "It's like one of those old movies where the girl's an heiress who gets into all sorts of trouble. Except Sheila already inherited and she doesn't get into trouble."

"That's me. The boring heroine of a non-screwball, non-comedy." I grinned.

He gave half a smile. It didn't improve my comfort level with him.

"What were your dreams before you inherited this life of leisure?"

"Nobody said this was a life of leisure. It's hard work finding things to fill your day. Unless, of course, you spend all day at the dog park—" I added a pointed look to drive home that my words applied to him. "—with your fellow life of leisure livers."

The smile grew to full. "Fair enough. I have a partial life of leisure because I'm a substitute teacher."

"Isn't it wonderful?" Clara crooned, "You're both high school teachers?"

I chose English teacher as my supposed former job, because I figured an English degree, especially fortified by fifteen years around books—though not actually writing them—should get me close enough to pass as knowledgeable. Plus, most people would shy away from discussing that profession too much—afraid of having their grammar corrected and/or reliving high school nightmares.

Not Teague O'Donnell. Lucky me.

"It is wonderful," he said to Clara, with no apparent sarcasm, much less smart-ass-ism. To me, he said, "Miss it?"

For a second, I thought about my old life.

Did I miss it?

But he didn't mean the *Abandon All* life. He meant my fictional teaching career.

"No. I guess I wasn't one of those natural teachers you read about. The kind who'd keep teaching even if they won the lottery." Time to get off the defensive. "You must understand how I feel, since you're not teaching full-time."

"Oh," Clara struck in, as if protecting a baby bird. "It's hard to get hired on in this district."

He lifted a shoulder. "My timing's bad. Moved here after the term started. Lots of folks signed up ahead of me."

"But that's wonderful," Clara said. If you've noticed she says lots of things are wonderful, you're right. And she meant it. "You and Murphy will have more time to bond here at the dog park."

"How'd you get Murphy?" I asked, welcoming this new topic.

"He showed up at my old place during a thunderstorm, shivering, wet, and demanding to be let in. No tags. I tried ads in the paper and called around to vets, but nobody seemed to be missing him. When I moved here, he came along."

"Why'd you move here?"

"Better weather," he said, deadpan. I had to give him credit. It's not easy to stay deadpan with sleet whizzing past your eyes.

"Where'd you live before? The North Pole?"

"Close. Outside Chicago. How about you?"

"New York."

"So, this is better weather for her, too." Clara might have volunteered that to soften the clipped edges of my response. "She's been out every day with Gracie. Well, almost every day. Except like yesterday, because she was meeting a contractor. She's fixing up the old house she bought, bringing it back to its old glory, and making her neighbors so happy."

This topic I'd happily elaborate on, since it took us away from my past and provided lots of detours. "My neighbors better wait to see what I actually accomplish before they get too happy. I waited all day yesterday for that contractor and he never showed up. Not to mention *contractor* is an elaborate name for what I hope he'll do—bookshelves in my office and shelves in the master bedroom closet—if he ever shows up."

"If you're not looking for fine carpentry, I could help you out," Teague said. "I'm pretty good with my hands."

Clara tried to hide laughter with coughing, which only drew more attention to her laughter at his innocent phrase.

It had been innocent, hadn't it?

Concentrating on ignoring Clara, I asked, "You can build shelves? Fine carpentry is definitely not necessary, especially in the closet, where I want shelves to hold up my shoes."

"Shoes? That changes everything." More deadpan. "Above my skill level with all the extra support, special bracing needed."

"Ha. Ha. Don't tell me you buy into the stereotype of a woman who overindulges in shoes."

"You don't overindulge in shoes?"

"Oh, yes, I do. I just don't want to be stereotyped. My vice is my personal vice, not a gender one."

That set Clara off into more coughing.

He might have caught a case of tact from her cough, because he said mildly, "I'd be happy to look at the job and give you a quote."

"You're not willing to do the work as a friend?"

"Who said we're friends?"

"Good point. Now I can say no thanks and give the job to someone else without compunction."

He nodded. "Compunction-free."

We set a time for him to come to my house the day after tomorrow in the morning. Unless he got called to substitute.

"You can bring Murphy." The impulsive words felt right as I heard them coming out of my mouth. What little we knew of each other was as dog owners. Why not keep it that way?

"I don't usually bring my dog to job sites."

"This isn't heavy construction. It's putting up a few shelves. In fact, it's just for you to give me a bid. Besides, Gracie would love it."

Was I being a wimp? I mean about catering to my dog's enjoyment. Trying to curry her favor by going to the dog park in the worst weather and now by providing her a playmate along with a construction project consultation.

On the other hand, it kept a buffer between the humans. Sure, I'd pay him to build bookshelves and even exchange a little banter, but I was in no position to get too friendly with a guy who actually knew stuff about my fictional occupation.

"Okay, I'll bring Murphy. You know, it seems like we have a lot in common," he said.

"Do we?" I asked at my most repressive.

Clara looked at me in surprise. I hadn't previously pulled out my repertoire of reactions learned and employed as the author of *Abandon All.*

Oh, except with the contractor who supposedly wanted to do work for me but showed up for one out of three appointments.

But my tone didn't daunt Teague O'Donnell. "We're both new to town, both have rescue dogs, both crazy enough to be out here today. Plus, you retired from teaching high school and I retired to teach high school."

Two could play the question game. "What did you retire fr—?"

My question disappeared in an eruption of barking.

CHAPTER THREE

BOB AND DWIGHT were arguing again and their dogs didn't like it, expressing their displeasure loudly this time.

All three of us turned. Teague also slid off the table.

"Watch the dogs," Clara recommended. "Ours still aren't worried."

She was right. They were head-down, all three noses sniffing the same half inch of ground, off to our right.

Teague stopped, still focused on the men.

Clara and I exchanged looks as we tried to decipher the topic of this dispute. They were plenty loud enough to be heard, but they kept talking—shouting—over each other. The dogs' barking added in made it hard.

Bob said something, then flipped at Dwight's scarf, setting the fringe to dancing.

"Oh, my God," Clara breathed. "He's gone mad."

I half expected Dwight to snatch the cap—bought in England, I'd already heard three times—off Bob's head.

"Shut up!" Dwight roared.

Everyone stared at him, including his dog and Bob's. Even our three dogs raised their heads and faced the commotion.

Berrie came toward the fence separating the enclosures. In the parking lot, Ronald turned from where he'd loaded the shelter dog into his vehicle.

No one made a sound.

The only one not quelled was Bob.

"…and if you knew half as much about dogs as you're pretending to, you'd know a dog can never appropriately be reprimanded by someone standing behind him."

Then Bob's finger jabbed at Dwight's chest, which was brave, if stupid, considering Dwight was half a foot taller than him and twice as brawny. "You are not fit to have responsibility for a dog. You have far to come to deserve the lowliest mongrel. Your whole family—"

Dwight knocked Bob's arm away with an angry swipe, nearly knocking Bob over. Not so much from the force as the unbalancing.

"They're getting riled," Clara muttered, still focused on the dogs. "Skeeter's confused, but Trevalyn's on alert. They're thinking about protecting their people."

Bob righted himself and continued the motion to push at Dwight's chest. Possibly caught by surprise, the bigger man stumbled back two steps, then a third when his foot slipped.

For half a second it seemed the end. Neither man moved. The dogs quieted.

Then Dwight's gloved hands fisted. Trevalyn growled low. Dwight started forward.

Clara and I moved, but well before we reached the combatants, Teague was there. Not directly between the other two men, but sort of bumping and maneuvering them farther and farther away from each other. His extended arm made light, intermittent contact with Bob's chest—almost like he was checking in. His opposite forearm came up and back toward Dwight's throat—when he wasn't staying out of Dwight's reach.

He kept talking, strong and calm. Almost like nonsense syllable to a baby. "No, no." "That's right." "Okay. Good." "Never mind that."

Dwight would step to the side and Teague would shift, still in a position to land a nasty blow to Dwight's throat.

Bob presented no threat, standing still and passively accepting Teague O'Donnell's contacts.

Then Teague said, "You're upsetting your dogs."

Bob immediately looked to Trevalyn, taking hold of the tweed collar that matched a custom tweed leash, murmuring would-be calming words in a shaky voice.

Dwight glared at Teague, almost appearing prepared to transfer the fight.

My chest hurt from holding my breath before Dwight finally stepped back and raised his hands.

"I don't need this. None of it." He started for the gate.

Skeeter gave Bob a long look, then around at all of us before slowly following his owner. At the concrete, Skeeter paused for the muddy paw-cleaning Dwight always did with a piece of toweling, but Dwight was too upset to bother.

And that was it, except for Dwight banging the gate closed behind himself and his dog.

"Bob, Bob, are you okay?" Berrie called from the other enclosure.

"Of—" He cleared his throat and started again. "Of course I am. I simply did what needed doing, standing up for the truth."

"I'm so glad you did. I've always said, under his butter-wouldn't-melt-in-his-mouth-act, Dwight Yagos is a bully."

"He's not," Clara said. "You don't agree on training dogs. Doesn't make either of you a bully. Each of you loves your dog."

"So says the friend to all, Clara Woodrow," sneered Bob. "But I know why you've made friends with this newcomer. I know."

He gave a hiccupping kind of laugh. He might have meant it to be sardonic. He actually sounded like a Minion from the *Despicable* movies.

I suspected reaction was setting in as Bob's adrenaline ebbed and he realized how close he'd come to one of Dwight's big fists.

"Oh, dear. Look at the time," he said, without, in fact, looking at the time. "I must go. I'll be late for an appointment if I don't leave right now."

The contractors I'd dealt with could learn a lot from Bob about promptness.

That thought didn't distract me from noticing Dwight's vehicle pull out of the lot, spewing gravel with its turn onto the highway. Coincidence that Bob had to leave only after that departure? I didn't think so.

Bob's hands shook as he put Trevalyn's tweed leash—lead, according to him—on and led him to the gate without another word to any of us, including Berrie, who clucked concern over him as he entered the vestibule. He left quickly.

Berrie immediately came to the point closest to where we all still stood.

"There's going to be bloodshed. Mark my words."

Teague's head came up, looking at her.

"You might well stare. But it's the truth. I have a client coming tomorrow who had actually considered talking to Dwight. I told her straight out what a horrible mistake that would be for her dog. Thank heavens she listened to me."

I'd heard the rumor from a couple people at the dog park that Berrie was setting herself up as a self-described trainer. She had a website. It didn't look half bad, actually. But I found myself muttering "Oh, brother" as I read her treatise on how one should never use the word leash, because a lead allows the owner to lead the dog, but with a leash the dog leads the owner. That was a whole lot of power to put into which word you used for a length of rope, leather, or plastic.

As far as anyone knew at the dog park, Berrie's only training consisted of listening to Bob pontificate. Her website listed no bona fides.

"It's a crime," she continued, "nobody has done anything about Dwight and the so-called dog people who follow his backward ways. Oh, I know what you have to say, Clara. But you're being a Pollyanna. I'm telling you, with that Dwight Yagos allowed to run free, there will be bloodshed."

"Oh, no," Clara said cheerfully and in contradiction to her earlier comments. "They huff and they puff, but nothing ever comes of it. You know, Berrie. Been that way for years."

"This—today—has changed things. You mark my words." Berrie ostentatiously turned her back on us and went to the enclosure's far side.

"*Was* this like all the other times?" Teague asked Clara.

She bit at her chapped lip. "They *do* huff and puff. But both of them seemed, um, edgier this time. Bob's always quick to point out fault, but he usually restrains himself more. And Dwight's usually slower to retaliate. Neither one of them was himself today. They were probably more irritable because of the weather."

CHAPTER FOUR

MY FIFTEEN YEARS as the supposed author of a milestone novel left gaps in my practical experience.

Grocery shopping, for instance.

I first tried to fill that gap with a day-time trip to the supermarket outside Haines Tavern.

The store had been filled with people who knew what they were doing and were intent on doing it as fast as possible. I've been on more TV talk shows than I can name, but that grocery store trip intimidated the heck out of me.

Since then, I'd been making night-time trips. Slowly feeling my way into the world of groceries.

One of the first things Great-Aunt Kit did after buying the brownstone in the Upper West Side we'd shared, was to employ a housekeeper/cook who also did the shopping.

"Grocery shopping is one of those unrewarding, repetitive exercises, like cleaning, that make no sense to do yourself if you can get out of it," she'd declared.

"Unrewarding? You have a clean house or you have food to make meals," I'd argued. Not that I really knew, since I'd gone from home to college to the brownstone, but opposing opinions were like catnip to Kit. "Those are rewards."

"Hah. And then you have to do them again and again and again. They never *stay* done. Not like writing a book. Once you've written it, it's written."

"But then you go and write another book."

"Precisely. A new, different book, with different characters, telling a different story. And once told, you go onto yet another new one. But with shopping and cleaning, you do the same thing over and over. They're only ever temporarily done."

"Laundry, too, I suppose?"

"Exactly," she'd said with approval.

Now, holding a large yellow onion in each hand, I smiled at the memory.

"You could take both." The male voice was close enough to stir the hair over my ear.

I spun to face the owner of the voice, but only made it partly around before my left arm encountered a solid wall. The jolt popped the onion out of that hand. I grabbed for it. Unfortunately, I grabbed for it with my right hand, which still held its own onion.

Right onion squirted loose, knocking left onion's orbit askew and out of the intersecting range of either of my hands.

A large male hand came in from the left and grabbed that onion. Another hand cupped my right elbow and partially straightened it, extending my hand like a net under someone jumping from a burning building. The second onion plopped into it.

Onion-geddon averted.

But I now had an unknown male draped around me like a shawl.

It tried to shrug off the shawl.

It didn't budge.

But after a slight pause, the man backed up.

I turned. The face was familiar, but…

Then I recognized the green jacket.

Murphy's human. Without the hood, scarf, and gloves, he somehow looked taller and broader.

"Didn't mean to startle you," Teague O'Donnell said with the half-smile that unsettled me earlier today. It did the same thing now. That smile seemed to say he knew things. He couldn't possibly, but still…

He handed me the left-handed onion. On the return trip, his hand took a detour, seeming to hover over my hair.

I stepped back. "What are you doing?"

"You look a lot better than you did at the dog park."

"Gee, thanks." I bit off *Right back at you* before it escaped.

That flustered him a bit. "Sorry. Your hair. You had some hair messed up. Probably from the hood…" Or maybe he pretended to be flustered, because he recovered awfully fast. "You shouldn't hide it by tying your hood tight."

"It was sleeting."

"Uh-huh."

He cleared his throat and I realized there'd been a long pause. "Why were you smiling at the onions?" he asked.

"Memories."

His mouth quirked. "About onions?"

"Yes." The single word and tone should close that door. "And I need to finish shopping if I want to make more memories. See you the day after tomorrow."

With a cool smile, I moved on.

We didn't cross paths again.

CHAPTER FIVE

THE NEXT DAY, I had a couple errands to run on the way to the dog park. Why don't you come along and see where I moved to, a town named Haines Tavern, Kentucky.

In writing fiction, it's called establishing the normal world.

In *A Christmas Carol*, that's Scrooge being, well, a Grinch. And in *Grinch*, that's the Grinch being a Scrooge. In the first *Star Wars* it's Luke Skywalker's life down on the farm or up on the farm. It's also life down on the farm for Dorothy in *The Wizard of Oz*.

Aunt Kit taught me all that.

So, here's my new normal world.

I backed out of my attached garage. The garage was of much more recent vintage than the house, but nicely done, including sitting back from the house's Georgian façade—a supporting cast member giving front-of-stage to the star.

The garage represented the one area I didn't have plans to work on. The rest would take time.

Continuing to back up the car, I bypassed dead, thorny branches of overgrown rosebushes on the left—hoping they were winter dead and would come back in the spring—and tried to ignore the expectant gaze of my dog in the rearview mirror.

I knew disappointment was coming her way and felt guilty. Dogs do not understand the value of delayed gratification.

Our routine of the past month included walks for her, interviewing contractors for me, trips to the dog park for her, yoga for me, chewing on toys for her, planning improvements on the house for me, checking out the window for potential marauders for her, talking on the phone with various family members for me, creating nose art on every window in the house for her, attending lectures at the County Extension office to learn about caring for the flora lurking under dead leaves and frost for me...

It's exactly the contrast I wanted from the previous fifteen years. Pleasant, quiet, serene, even a little boring.

I know, I know. I never should have even thought that last part.

It was an invitation to trouble.

Because here's the thing about setting up the normal life in fiction—it's the precursor to knocking that poor protagonist for one heck of a loop.

By a ghost and three spirits, by the true Christmas spirit of the Whos, by a galactic war, by a tornado. Our hero—ahem, or heroine—is about to have normal smashed to smithereens.

GRACIE SLUMPED IN the back seat when we turned right instead of left at the first stop sign.

She already knew left meant the dog park. *Good.*

Right meant something other than the dog park. *Bad.*

Gracie and I are past the initial getting-to-know-you stage, but I catch myself now and then looking at her and thinking, *Holy smokes, I'm totally responsible for this creature.*

Yes, a lot of people my age—mid-thirties—are responsible for a number of creatures, including little human ones. But during my *Abandon All* years, I didn't do any of the pairing up into a couple and starting a family that often occurs during those years. So this was new for me.

I prepared for it by researching.

Not only did I do considerable research in college, but in the years with Kit, I added a virtual Ph.D.

I tagged along while she did background training, interviews, and road trips for whatever she wrote. It was a necessity for the follow-up books to *Abandon All.* I could better pretend to be their mother since

I'd been present during their gestation.

Besides, it was fun, so I did it for all her books, especially enjoying the background work for her mysteries.

So, naturally, my preparation to adopt a rescue dog included research. I read about the importance of bonding with the animal. One blogger wrote about how she went a week without bathing to imprint her scent on the animal.

Phew! I bet it imprinted on the dog. And anybody else within a mile.

Before I gave up showers, however, a footnote said the blogger returned the animal because they weren't on the same wavelength.

Sometimes I wished the dogs got to vote on who adopted them.

When I was a kid, my family had Bounce, a golden retriever. Lovable, loving, amiable, and not the brightest. He would have imprinted with a rock. He certainly bonded with my stuffed caterpillar named Wombat. Bounce took over Wombat his first day in the house. We'd find the increasingly woebegone Wombat in drawers, under the bed, behind doors, nestling in potted plants, and sitting in Bounce's water dish. We buried Wombat with him.

Gracie was decidedly more emotionally cautious than Bounce.

Not me. I was the human version of Bounce.

I took one look at Gracie on the collie rescue website and I forgot every other breed, mix, and unknown I'd looked at. I was smitten. Not with *a* collie. With *this* collie.

When I went to her foster home to meet her, my heart thudded hard with excitement.

The heart-thudding took on different cadences as I went through the vetting—no pun intended—process, including a home visit.

Then came the day I brought her home. When I invited her to jump into the back of my car, she gave her foster mother a long don't-make-me-do-this look. With tears in her eyes and voice, the woman said, "It's okay, Gracie. You'll be happy with Sheila. Good girl." Gracie didn't budge. "Get in the car, Gracie."

Without looking at me, Gracie obeyed the foster mom.

I talked to her throughout the drive to Haines Tavern. She looked out the window.

As I took her out of the car, I bent down to grab the bag of goodies the foster mother sent along and caught a whiff of the top of Gracie's head.

Corn chips.

If I wasn't already there, I fell irrevocably in love.

I'm not even that wild about corn chips. On her, though, the scent was irresistible.

I swear I've caught this dog looking at me with the flipped version of my *Holy smokes, I'm totally responsible for this creature* thought—that she's responsible for me.

Collies can be like that, according to my reading. They're bred to watch over the flock. If you become their flock, get ready to be watched.

But Gracie has not fallen in love with me.

CHAPTER SIX

FIRST ERRAND STOP was the post office to mail a package of cookies to my great-aunt Kit.

Until the past few months, I'd periodically packaged up cookies and taken them to the madhouse post office in Manhattan to send to my family, while Kit ate them straight from the brownstone's kitchen.

Now, I took them along when I drove to visit my family every few weeks—we needed to talk about them coming to visit me—and mailed survival rations to Kit in North Carolina. Yes, she could get cookies in the Outer Banks, where she now lived, but not *my* caramel nut cookies.

From my point of view, it didn't hurt that I did the mailing from the Haines Tavern post office.

In dipping into the history of my new town, I'd learned the Haines Tavern post office started life as the first permanent house in the county. It also had been the first Haines' tavern, barn, and stable.

It became the post office well after Hezekiah Haines built a second, significantly larger, brick structure as his home, tavern, and lodging rooms—with separate barn and stable, the height of poshness.

The post office sat in the center of one of the four blocks facing the town square. Next to it was the town's branch of the county library. On its other side sat another historic building, which housed a combination hardware and feed store. That might sound like it ruined the charm of the town square, but the frontage on the square retained its historic appearance, while the business end of hardware and feed faced the back, with the entrance from a side street.

The Historic Haines Tavern—every written reference included the word historic, always capitalized—occupied the square frontage at right angles to the post office and its companions. This was the second of Hezekiah's buildings. The tavern sat in the middle with a set-back patio and deck flanking it for summer seating, then gardens, all enclosed by a tidy fence replicating the one in a 19th nineteenth century painting of the Historic Haines Tavern, available as postcards, prints, and placemats.

Next around the square came two churches sitting side-by-side— First Church of Haines Tavern and First Church of North Bend County. Someday, I wanted to learn the history of those two buildings. I had an image of a race to finish first that left John Henry in the dust.

The county courthouse occupied the fourth side of the square, directly across from the tavern. That had to be convenient in earlier times when people got drunk at the tavern and could be marched straight across to the courthouse, which also served as the jail.

Now Historic Haines Tavern's main business was serving meals, with the bar mostly for waiting for a table. And the current jail was about a mile away, near the dog park.

Of course, in the center, sat the town square and at its center rose a fountain. I looked forward to seeing it running when the weather turned warm. I also had hopes for the square's four corners, which promised gardens in the spring.

Today, they were slushy, sodden messes.

Oh, yes, it would be another fine day at the dog park.

But, first, the post office.

"GOOD MORNING, SHEILA."

"Hi, Ruby."

Ruby Zweydorf had called me by name since my first trip to the post office and insisted I reciprocate. Nobody was a stranger to Ruby. Including my dog. "You didn't bring our sweet girl Gracie in today? Leave her at home?"

The Haines Tavern, Kentucky, post office might have influenced my decision to buy the house I did.

As I mentioned, this normal world is all pretty new to me.

The first time I saw the post office, on the way to viewing the house, it was decorated for Christmas, exactly the way a tiny brick historical building should be decorated. With deep red ribbons on real evergreen wreaths hung on the central door and in each of the two narrow windows on either side of it.

Now firmly into February, I missed the decorations, but the elfin proportions still made the building cute.

Ruby matched the proportions, except for her outsized smile.

"Gracie's in the car," I said. "We're on our way to the dog park, but needed to mail this first."

"More cookies?" She didn't wait for an answer. "But why didn't you bring Gracie in?"

"Uh, that customer of yours wasn't too happy last time I did. Said it was against the law except for service dogs. I didn't want to risk causing a problem for you."

I was being discreet by not naming the customer who had objected vociferously to Gracie being in the post office a couple weeks ago. I'd been taken aback by his reaction. He knew Gracie from the dog park and certainly wasn't afraid of her.

"Pffft. I'd call Bob Coble a fussy old woman, but I won't insult old women. And I can handle any problem he tries to dish out."

Ruby clearly didn't consider discretion necessary in front of the gray-haired man sitting on a stool in the corner reading the newspaper. Come to think of it, I don't think I'd ever been in the post office when he wasn't there in the corner, behind a newspaper.

"Besides, this is *my* post office. Your Gracie is welcome any time, as sweet and well-behaved as she is."

Gracie *can* be sweet. Not all the time, but sometimes. As for well-behaved … call it a work in progress.

I suspected Gracie's behavior was bathed in the warm glow of nostalgia in Ruby's eyes. She'd told me her family had a beloved and amazing collie during her childhood.

"Though I can see why you didn't want to take the cookies to the dog park," she said. "Those dogs get one whiff of cookies and they'll all be fighting to get in your car. Works the same way on me. I know you pack these up real well, but I swear I can smell them."

I chuckled, and pulled out a baggie with three cookies from my pocket and placed it on the counter. "Can't have you getting in trouble for tampering with the mail."

"You are an *angel*." She scooped up the baggie in a nanosecond.

If Bob Coble saw this transaction, he'd probably report me for offering and Ruby for accepting a bribe to a postal employee. Especially if he ever saw Gracie come inside again.

He certainly couldn't complain when Ruby charged and I paid the full rate to get these cookies to Aunt Kit.

"You bring Gracie in next time," Ruby said as I prepared to leave. "I've taken care of Bob Coble."

I waved and went next door to the library, dropping off two movies on DVD and a tome on home renovations and repair. I picked up three more books on the topic—my head was going to explode soon—another on dogs, a trio of back issue magazines, and two more movies to supplement the ebook fiction I read.

"I swear your house already looks better," Amy Kackley, the woman behind the checkout counter said to me.

I could have checked out electronically, but it doesn't always work with the DVDs. Besides, I'd seen Amy and wanted to say hello for entirely selfish reasons.

Donna introduced us a few weeks ago in the hardware store. Amy lived at the other end of the block from me and I often encountered her on walks with Gracie. Every time we spoke, she had something nice to say about the house. I couldn't resist the boosts.

"I haven't had a chance to do much outside," I demurred.

The first priorities included replacing the roof, then repairing and painting the exterior trim.

The kitchen and bathrooms functioned. Updating them would come later. The floors were solid, but needed refinishing. Raised seams under the paint revealed its neutral colors covered wallpaper.

"Sometimes a house perks up, like it knows somebody's taking an interest. Heading to the dog park?"

"We are. Gracie's in the car."

"I wish I could go during the workday when it's not as crowded. Though, I hear that means you're more likely to be the target for that demagogue."

Since I didn't know whether she meant Dwight or Bob, I stuck with, "Gracie loves having lots of room to run."

"Well, I see you have lots more hard work ahead of you." She nodded toward my checked-out stack. "The house is going to love it and so am I, watching everything you do."

I left the library with a heavy load but lighter spirits.

Back at the car, Gracie spun around in the back seat excitedly.

I didn't fool myself it was for me. She was sure she knew where we were going next.

And she was right.

CHAPTER SEVEN

Even with the errand-running, we reached the dog park ahead of Clara and LuLu, which threatened to send my dog into apoplexy.

As soon as I saw the SUV pulling in, I had Gracie out and ready to go. She was done with being patient.

I sprung the good news on Clara as soon as her door opened. "The mud's going to be even worse today."

"We could go in the other section."

"Berrie's there."

She backed out of where she'd been hooking LuLu to her leash and stared. "In a large-dog area?"

LuLu took the opening to jump down without permission and greet Gracie with mutual, prancing circles.

"She and the Bostons are with somebody with a large dog—a German shepherd."

Clara rolled her eyes as she closed up the SUV. "Who's she lecturing this time?"

"I didn't recognize it."

It was not a veiled slap at the woman with Berrie, but referring to the German shepherd.

Dogs were easier to identify than owners. They didn't change clothes and rarely adopted a new hairstyle. Plus, there was frequently someone shouting their name, a great memory aid.

"Doesn't look happy in there with Berrie," Clara said with a hint of satisfaction as she scanned the enclosure Ronald had used yesterday.

That was one of the elements that saved Clara from being just too nice.

Her observation was accurate. She didn't look happy. She looked cowed—the owner, not the dog.

As we approached the vestibule, any hope that being in a different enclosure would deter Marcus from his usual demonstration evaporated.

He zipped from the far end to the gate, starting his noise well before he arrived. The Bostons brigade came after him.

The shepherd tried to resist.

His head swiveled from the gate to his owner and back.

But after thirty seconds of head-swiveling, it was too much for him.

He jumped up from a sit, turning toward the gate in mid-air and added his thunderous bark to the melee.

"Do you mind!" Berrie shouted. "You're interrupting a lesson."

"As if it's our fault," Clara grumbled. I barely heard her.

Clara and I made our dogs sit and stay while we removed their leashes, then we released them into the enclosure. It was always a close-run thing of whether we could get out "okay" before they disappeared. Today was a little easier than yesterday. Today there were no other dogs in the enclosure to lure them.

Also, no Bob, no Dwight, not even Teague O'Donnell.

I was right. The mud was much worse from the overnight precipitation, which had shifted from sleet to snow sometime after Gracie went out for the last time, based on the patches in my back yard this morning.

"Look at them go—joy in motion." Clara yanked her hood back into place, and shifted back to Topic A. "After yesterday, something has to be done about Dwight and Bob. Something has to change."

She was still rehashing it when we reached the picnic table. It was too wet to sit on today, but the wooden roof over it protected us some from the icy rain.

"And Berrie… Okay, okay, I know I shouldn't let her get to me. It's just hypocritical to critique other people's dogs when hers … And to yell at us on top of it." She waved a hand in front of her face as if to cool off, when the weather was doing it already.

"Uh-huh," I contributed.

"She's not really *that* bad. I mean, I know she's annoying, and I don't blame anyone else for feeling she's, well, pushy, or even—I don't want to say strident, because it's not like she's *horribly* loud, but so, uh, *forceful* in her opinions—not that she expresses them as opinions because she makes it sound like the great dog in the sky has filled her in on every secret of every canine that ever, well… And I will admit I was annoyed when she said LuLu would be better behaved if I improved my posture, but at her core she does love dogs."

I said nothing. Of course, I hadn't had much opportunity.

"Right?" Clara prompted.

"Sure."

She released a breath in a sigh. "I shouldn't be so hard on her. I get wound up. Like when people don't pick up their dog's poop or— well…"

"Or when they don't call it poop?"

Clara zeroed in on where LuLu was circling, mentally marking the location. "I see no need for coarseness," she said, reminding me she actually was a Southern lady.

She left the roof's protection on poop patrol.

I called after her, "Are you saying Donna telling me you went toe-to-toe with a guy last fall, accusing him of being a serial poop avoider, wasn't true?"

She stifled a chuckle and aimed for high dignity—as high as dignity could get when bending to pick up poop in a handy biodegradable bag currently over one hand like a very unappetizing oven mitt. When she finished picking up, she'd roll the bag down her hand, tie the ends, and drop it in the trash.

"I simply pointed out the error of his ways."

I laughed.

Then—and I can't tell you why—I turned my head toward the right.

The dogs had gone to that side of the enclosure, along the rise before the dip known as Las Vegas. Their movements suddenly became staccato, like they were walking on their toes. Gracie's ears pricked up, almost seeming to quiver with intense interest. They picked up their pace.

Then stopped abruptly.

Standing stock still at the highest spot in the park, just short of where the ground slid down toward out-of-sight Las Vegas.

Was that where they were looking? Or a bit farther to the fence? Or the trees on the other side? Even, mostly obscured even with the trees bare, to the sheriff's department and jail?

Gracie turned her head, looking around toward me and—I could swear—making eye contact despite the distance. She gave a single bark, turned back toward the outside fence, and trotted on, dropping out of sight.

"Clara," I called. "I think. … I think something's wrong."

She turned, following the direction of my gaze, just before LuLu, too, disappeared from sight.

"What—?"

A piercing, lamenting siren of a sound came that I had never heard before, yet knew it came from Gracie. A solo for the first long drawn-out note, before it was punctuated by LuLu's barks.

I was right. Something was wrong.

Clara was right, too. Something was going to have to be done. And something had changed.

Everything had changed.

The Dwights and Bobs war had a casualty.

CHAPTER EIGHT

CLARA, SEVERAL YARDS closer than I was, reached the ridge and stared down in the direction the dogs had gone.

Her jaw slackened, her eyes popped wide and staring.

"Oh, my God," she cried. "Oh, my God, oh, my God, oh, my God."

She started down toward the dogs, as they switched roles, with Gracie setting up a frenzy of barking, and LuLu emitting a chilling howl.

I realized I was running. I'd closed the gap some, but Clara had stopped well before I came up panting next to her.

Together, we looked down at the tumbled form clad in a cap, a jacket with hunters' shoulder blocks, and knee-high boots, all dusted by snow. What was not part of that signature look was the dog leash digging into the flesh of his neck.

Bob Coble.

Gracie circled the body, as if intent on herding the departed back into the land of the living. She barked in bursts of three, sharp and piercing sounds that communicated distress and alerted alarm, LuLu's deep woofing gave the staccato bursts of a bass line. She made dashes toward the corpse, peeling away well before reaching it, in order to retreat behind the perimeter circle Gracie had created, then building her courage and dashing in again.

There was a poop off to the side. Someone had stepped in it. Not the dogs. The smooshing was too complete.

"Oh my God, oh my God, oh my God."

I reached Clara as she would have stepped closer, one arm extended toward what had once been Bob Coble. I grasped her other arm and held on.

"Don't. Clara, don't. We can't—we shouldn't touch anything."

I waited a moment, partly to let the words sink in, partly to steady my breathing coming in gasps hard enough to shake my ribcage.

"This is … This is so—It's—"

"Murder. He's been murdered."

Clara let out a sound that stopped and quieted both dogs.

I called Gracie to me, knowing LuLu would follow. Gracie paused, appearing to assess where her loyalties lay.

She opted for the living, and came to me.

Holding on to Clara's arm, I backed us both up several yards. As I'd hoped, Gracie followed, leading LuLu, too.

I leashed Gracie, then, taking the leash from Clara's limp hand, secured LuLu. I started our group toward the entrance.

Turning our backs to the body seemed to break the spell for Clara.

"We have to do something. Oh, Sheila, we have to do *something*."

"We have to call the police. That's what we have to do. Do you have your phone on you?"

"No."

"Me, either. We have to go back to the cars."

"But, he might still be—"

"No." Not with that face. Not with the way the dogs reacted.

I tucked a hand under Clara's elbow and hurried her out of the enclosure, past Marcus' ruckus, and Berrie's glower at us, though she never stopped talking at the German shepherd owner.

We all got into Clara's SUV, with both dogs in back, lying up against each other and watching us. I sat in the passenger seat and called 911.

I had to repeat what I said a couple times.

Then we waited.

It wouldn't take long, considering how close the sheriff's department was. But they had to come by road, which added distance.

Clara, clearly shaken, sputtered in half sentences and questions.

I listened, but had no answers.

What kept running through my head was Clara no longer had to worry about a petition. One of her bad influences wasn't ever coming back to the Torrid Avenue Dog Park.

CHAPTER NINE

I FELT SORRY for Berrie.

She was our proof we'd just arrived at the dog park. With virtually no opportunity to slip the snap end of a leash through the loop handle and pull and pull and pull until it stopped Bob Coble's life.

She, however, had no witness that the huddled, mottle-faced body had been there, hidden from her sight by the drop down to the creek, when she'd arrived.

No one had been there when she arrived, she'd said, though Augustine Lorenson and her dog, Dieter, arrived only a few minutes after her.

Why did she use the enclosure furthest from the crime scene instead of her usual one?

Nobody asked her, though, amid questions about the sequence of arrivals.

Berrie and the Bostons.

Augustine and the German shepherd, Dieter.

Me and Gracie.

Clara and LuLu.

I couldn't even begin to imagine how many times Berrie said it, considering how many times I'd repeated my account to a rotating cast of deputies.

When did I move here? From where? I gave my parents' address, which had been my official address for a few months. If they dug deeper, though, that would open the proverbial can of worms.

Apparently I'd finally repeated it enough. Because they told me to stay by Deputy Eckles, who was questioning Berrie—again—not far from the PortaPotty and faucet.

Clara was on the far side of the parking lot, with the German shepherd's owner a short distance away, along with more deputies. All the dogs had been secured in vehicles, with Gracie and LuLu still together in the back of Clara's SUV.

After the first round of official vehicles arrived, I saw Teague and Murphy pulled in. As a couple more dog park people arrived, I saw him keep them a good distance away. Then, as more official vehicles came, his vehicle was hemmed in. I'd seen him questioned by a deputy taking notes, then a second deputy, checking something on his car's computer. Who knew how many others in between.

Beyond the outer ring of official vehicles, I spotted Ronald, Donna, and a few other dog park regulars. I was most surprised to see Ruby from the post office and Amy from the library. Ruby had said she didn't have a dog, since her aged Yorkie died in the fall. Amy didn't have her English setter mix with her, which made sense since it was the middle of her work day.

The one person I didn't see I might have expected was Dwight Yagos. At one point, I thought I caught a flash of UK blue, but that could have been anybody.

"Did you see anyone go into that enclosure before the other two ladies arrived?" Deputy Eckles asked Berrie.

Her eyes darted to me, then away.

"They didn't arrive together."

"Oh?"

I sure hoped the deputy was acting uninformed in an effort to elicit more information, and not because he'd forgotten I'd told him at least twenty-seven times that I'd arrived before Clara.

Hoped, but didn't count on it.

"I was aware of a car arriving first. A sedan," she added as if not owning a SUV, van, or station wagon constituted dog abuse.

"Uh-huh." He added a squiggle to his notebook. "Did you notice a time?"

"No, but it was several minutes before the other vehicle arrived."

C'mon, Berrie, come out and say it was plenty of time for me to go in, kill Bob Coble and return to the parking lot to be there when Clara showed up.

It hadn't been. But she could pretend.

Plus, there was a major flaw with her making that accusation—and it wasn't that I would have needed to break land speed records to accomplish the task.

"How much time."

"I can't say. I wasn't paying attention to that. I was concentrating on working with Dieter."

"Dieter?"

"The shepherd."

The deputy glanced around and frowned. I feared he was looking for a guy in a robe with a crooked stick.

"The German shepherd," Berrie said with sharp impatience. She pointed to a van. "I was working with the shepherd and his owner, Augustine Lorenson."

"Yeah, okay. But you had a good view of the parking lot and the gates."

"I. Was. Working. The. Dog." She stretched the gaps between words so you could hear the subtext of *You blithering, idiot.*

"But you could see the gates."

"I *could*, but I wasn't looking at them. When I'm working a dog, a marching band could go by and I wouldn't notice."

"Ms. Mackey could have gone into that enclosure and you wouldn't have known?"

"I would say—"

She broke off before the *yes* already visible in her face became a spoken word.

Not from an attack of conscience, but because Clara had broken free of her deputy handler across the parking lot, and was charging toward us, with her hold on the German shepherd's owner's arm overcoming the woman's clear reluctance.

"Berrie, you stop being spiteful because Sheila told you no thank you to all that unwanted advice you're forever handing out. I heard you from over there and you tell this deputy the truth—"

Berrie gasped in outrage, which left her at a disadvantage when she tried to shout, "How dare you" because she didn't have enough breath, having gasped it away.

Clara steamed on. "There is no way on this earth Sheila could have gone into that gate without Marcus raising a fuss—"

"I was focused on the shepherd. I wouldn't have heard anyth—"

"Baloney. And besides—" She spun around to the other woman, Augustine Lorenson. "—did you hear Marcus carrying on? Barking and barking and running around in circles and usually the other Bostons join in."

"No, but—" started the shepherd's hapless owner.

"See!" Clara declared triumphantly to both Deputy Eckles and Deputy Hensen, who'd followed Clara over. He'd been one of my earlier questioners.

"Hold up there. Before we get into that—" I had the impression Deputy Eckles wanted to get away from the subject of dogs. "—let me ask you all together now, did Bob Coble have any enemies?"

That stopped the conversation.

It wasn't the old *Don't speak ill of the dead* shutting us up.

Berrie was probably trying to grapple with the concept anyone could not adore Bob.

I suspected Clara, like me, was doing the math.

If you figured half the people coming to the dog park were neutral, then the other half divided into Dwights and Bobs, that left a quarter of the people who came here who actively loathed Bob. All the Dwights.

Augustine Lorenson was probably trying to figure out how she'd been lucky enough to pick today to get "instruction" from Berrie Vittlow.

"Well?" Eckles prodded.

The other deputy, I noticed, was watching all of us carefully. I tried to make my face as devoid of thought—or math—as possible.

Berrie broke the silence with a single, screeched word. "Dwight!"

"Dwight?" Eckles repeated without comprehension.

"Dwight killed him! Bob, oh, Bob. My God, I knew Dwight was a spiteful, jealous low-life, of course, but never, ever, ever did I think he'd actually—"

"Dwight who? Why would he kill, uh…"

"Bob Coble," the other deputy supplied.

"Why this Dwight?" Eckles pretended he hadn't heard Hensen, which also allowed him to pretend he hadn't needed the insert.

"Because he hated him. Because Bob was magnificent with dogs. Knew them inside and out, knew how to *communicate* with them, firm and in charge, but so kind because everything he did was for their own good. But *Dwight* was a pretender. A nobody who bumbled around claiming he knew something when he knew nothing and he couldn't bear that. So he killed—*Killed.* Oh my God, he *murdered* Bob." She wailed.

Deputy Eckles shouted over her, wisely addressing Clara and me. "Dwight, was he here today?"

"We didn't see him." Clara gestured to include me and our dogs.

The other deputy gave me a questioning look. "Didn't see him or anyone except the people you've seen," I confirmed.

I didn't think that helped one iota to clear Dwight, however.

Because Bob's body had been there for a while.

That conclusion was not based on any observation of rigor mortis—my research with Kit had never been that technical—but on the crust of undisturbed snow on Bob's distinctive jacket. That snow fell during the night.

I had no idea when Berrie arrived. Or her client. Only Berrie's word for it.

How long had she *really* been here?

The sheriff's department's experts would surely pin down how long Bob had been there far more firmly than my observations of snow did. Besides, I did not want to get into a discussion of how I might know about or happen to observe such things.

That connected too closely to Kit, *Abandon All,* and my past identity.

While I thought, Deputy Eckles asked Clara questions about Bob and Dwight. He wrapped up with, "So this Dwight Yagos and the victim were major rivals. But Dwight hasn't been seen at the dog park today by any of you folks who were here when the victim was found."

Berrie's voice vibrated in a mini-wail. "The *victim* … Of *murder*…"

Perhaps Eckles was simply trying to avoid eye contact with Berrie when he slid a glance toward me, but it was a tactical error.

Clara pounced.

"See? There? I *knew* you were falling for Berrie's baloney. You're thinking Sheila could have gone in and been back in time to be in her vehicle when I arrived without Berrie and Augustine noticing, but you're wrong. And I can prove it."

"Because of a dog barking?" Skepticism oozed into the deputy's placating. "Out here a dog barking is nothing unusual, and if these two ladies wouldn't have noticed, not to mention the dog might not have barked at all…"

Clara smirked at him. "Let's run an experiment. Put Berrie and Augustine in that enclosure, just like they were, with Marcus and Dieter and the other Bostons, and then we'll have Sheila go by, and we'll see what happens."

"That's absurd. There's no reason for me to do that," Berrie declared.

The deputy rubbed his chin. "No reason not to, either. It might not settle this one way or the other, but it could add more information."

My estimation of him jumped several levels.

Clara redirected her smirk at Berrie.

Berrie stopped protesting when she recognized the deputy was getting irked. Berrie could be annoying, but she wasn't stupid.

"So, if Sheila had gone past—but she didn't—which even if Berrie and Augustine were at the farthest corner of the section—Augustine says they weren't. They spent the whole time by the picnic table, right, Augustine?"

"Uh-huh," the woman said.

I wasn't sure how much stock the deputy put in that confirmation.

"Thank you, ma'am. I think we've got it covered. Hensen, you take Ms. Mackey back behind those vehicles, out of sight." Clara's mouth opened to inform him that wouldn't fool Marcus, but I caught her eye, and she fell silent, allowing the deputy to continue in peaceful ignorance. "When I signal, Ms. Mackey, I want you to walk back here, come into the main gate, then go on through the gate to the section where you found the body. But not off the concrete."

There was more to untangle—getting Marcus, finding the best disposition of Clara so she wouldn't skew the test. It was decided she would go with the deputies into the closer small-dog enclosure, but she was to be strictly silent.

Deputy Hensen and I reached a spot behind a forensics van. Its occupants were already deployed.

A dozen yards away, I saw Teague O'Donnell watching us closely.

Deputy Hensen spat onto the parking lot's stony surface. "Like that ol' dog doesn't know pre-*cise*-ly where you and me are this second—and where we've been the past two weeks."

"I take it Deputy Eckles isn't a dog person."

He grunted. "You could say that."

His radio produced the order, "Send her out. Alone."

Walking the narrow strip of empty parking lot toward the main gate, I felt as nervous and exposed as I had before the first interviews I did for *Abandon All*.

I lifted my head … and promptly stumbled against a raised portion of the concrete outside the main gate. I might have made a small noise, but it was lost in the squawk of the gate opening.

Immediately followed by a sound blending a bark and a banshee's wail, outdoing any siren ever invented. Marcus charged to the gate of the other large-dog enclosure. The humans thundered after him.

"Can you make him stop?" Deputy Eckles shouted. At least that's what I think he said. I'm not the best lip-reader.

"What?" Berrie shouted back. It required no lip-reading skill. She'd keep pretending she couldn't hear the request, because as long as she couldn't hear it, she didn't have to issue the command Marcus wouldn't obey, and she didn't have to admit she didn't have perfect control over her dog.

As tempting as watching farce was, my adrenaline was ebbing fast. I wanted to go home and pull the covers over my head. Possibly with Gracie there, too, despite my determination to not let her become a furniture dog.

I reached over the fence and put my hand on Marcus' blocky head.

"—and no way could Sheila have gone in there without Berrie and Augustine knowing," Clara shouted into sudden silence.

Eckles' eyes widened, then narrowed as he turned to me.

"All you had to do is touch him, and he quiets?"

"I have no idea. First time I tried it."

I took my hand off Marcus, pivoted and walked to the other enclosure's gate. Those four steps were accompanied by his guttural barks segueing toward banshee. With the gate closed, my back turned, and two steps in, Marcus stopped.

"—every time," Clara shouted. She barely dropped the volume as she added, "Until she's a couple feet inside the other area and turns her back."

"He gets over-excited around Sheila, that's all," Berrie said.

"Damnedest thing I ever heard," Deputy Hensen said, coming up. "What about when your dog's with you?"

"Same thing." I kept my back to Marcus.

"He doesn't react to me at all, with or without LuLu," Clara volunteered.

"Everyone says you arrived after Ms. Mackey," Eckles said politely. As if she'd be disappointed to be left out of contention for the role of potential murder suspect. "Ms. Mackey, do it again with your dog—if you're still willing to cooperate."

"Deputy, I'm eager to cooperate, to remove this red herring." Although I doubted anyone heard me, because with my return to the vestibule, Marcus launched into full volume again.

We repeated the exercise with Gracie on the leash by my side. Deputy Hensen showed his good sense by praising Gracie. She fluttered her tail, but was mostly focused on the strange happenings.

Eckles gestured to start and it was a repeat, with the addition of Gracie barking sharply at Marcus before I put a hand over the fence to turn off his canine blast.

This time Eckles was satisfied enough to order Berrie and me to put our dogs in our vehicles.

"Okay. Now, we're taking you all to the sheriff's department."

CHAPTER TEN

"**THEY WON'T LET** me call Ned." Clara's voice wavered.

The dogs moved restively, looking toward her from where they were lying under the sheriff's department conference table.

"Your husband?" Teague asked. She nodded. "They want to make sure they hear your freshest recollections. Once they get our statements, they'll either let us go, or make other arrangements."

At the calm in his voice, the dogs settled again. I didn't. I didn't like the sound of "make other arrangements."

After the announcement that we'd be coming to the sheriff's department, we'd asked to go home to leave our dogs and change.

Deputy Eckles wouldn't consider it.

His first choice was for deputies to drive us here in official cars, leaving our vehicles and dogs at the dog park.

We strenuously objected because of the cold, the upset to the dogs, and our lack of access to them. Especially since he couldn't or wouldn't tell us how long it would be before we could get back to them.

Then he agreed deputies would drive each of our vehicles with owners and dogs as passengers the short distance to the sheriff's department. But, appearing more disturbed by the idea of our dogs inside than he had by violent death, he wanted us to leave the dogs in the vehicles.

Starting with a dismissive, "I don't know about these other animals, but…" Berrie delivered a protracted lecture on Bostons' susceptibility to the cold because of their short, thin coats, and pug-like faces. She didn't say pug-like. I was sparing you the full explanation, which included words like brachycephalic.

Eckles was not spared. Yet, when I pointed out it wasn't any warmer in the sheriff's department parking lot than the dog park parking lot, I swear he liked that less than Berrie's lecture.

Some people don't appreciate logic.

In the end, our loud and long objections reached somebody higher up the command chain than Eckles. Somebody who liked dogs.

Berrie and the Bostons went into one room, while Clara, Teague, I, and our dogs were assigned to a conference room we were told was sometimes used by K-9 units and told to wait.

From the sniff-fest by the dogs, I believed the part about the K-9 units, especially when a deputy with "K-9" on his sleeve came in with a large bowl of water and petting and attention for each dog.

He left, but a silent deputy remained in the corner by the door. Watching and listening. Our guard lost a lot of imposing points when he clucked at and petted each of the dogs in turn.

"I don't understand why they're talking to Augustine first," Clara complained.

"She came after Berrie did and was with Berrie the whole time. They both say that," I said.

Clara snorted. "Berrie's so biased, she's not a good witness."

"They don't know that." Although they'd now heard it, thanks to our deputy in the corner.

"Oh, I suppose you're right." She chuckled slightly, with the tiniest undercurrent of hysteria. "It'll serve Deputy Eckles right, making Berrie wait."

Teague and I looked at her. I supposed the deputy in the corner did, too, but I wasn't watching him.

She continued, "Gracie, LuLu, and Murphy might leave some fur—"

No *might* about it. Tufts already decorated the industrial carpet.

"—but wait until Deputy Eckles tries to use whatever room they have Berrie's Boston terrier mob in."

I asked, "Why? They seem like good dogs."

"It's not that. Boston's fart a lot. They're notorious for it. You would not believe something that small could clear a room the way they can." Clara's chuckled again.

The deputy in the corner made a slight sound, but when we all turned toward him, he had his expression under control, showing nothing.

"I once went to a meeting about the dog park at Berrie's, back when we had flooding from the creek, and it was the most efficient meeting I have *ever* been to. Nobody wanted to stay a minute longer than necessary."

We all chuckled slightly, but it didn't completely remove the tension from the room.

"You'll probably be the next to leave," I said to Teague. "In fact, I don't understand why you're here at all."

The deputy in the corner scratched his nose.

Teague shrugged. "Guess it was the timing of my arrival."

I opened my mouth to say he'd arrived not only after we'd found the body, but after the first deputies, so that didn't explain their interest in him.

Then closed it. And said instead, "Clara, if they give us a choice, you go before me. I don't have any place to be. But Ned will worry if you're not home when he gets there."

"They probably won't give us a choice," Teague said.

That seemed rather pessimistic. Though I understood his mood, because I shared it.

"But you do have somewhere to be, Sheila," Clara said. "You have bunco tonight."

"I totally forgot." My neighbor, the librarian Amy, invited me as a substitute and I'd hoped it would be a good way to get to know more people.

Mind you, I've never played the game.

The only thing I knew was the phrase Bunco Squad, which made me a bit uneasy. After all, police departments don't have a Jigsaw Puzzle Squad or a Scrabble Unit.

Wanting to know what I was getting into. I looked it up.

It started in England as a gambling game similar to three-card Monte, traveled to San Francisco in the 1850s for the post-Gold Rush. Turned respectable for several decades, then resurfaced for gambling in the Roaring Twenties, giving its name to law enforcement fighting fraud as the Bunco Squad, before a dose of obscurity ... until the past few decades.

Reassurance came when I read that most people play now for a fun and easy excuse to get together with friends to eat and drink a little, while talking a lot.

The talk tonight would surely center on the murder of Bob Coble. Instead of my getting to know neighbors, they'd try to get all the details of the scene at the dog park out of me.

"Maybe I should cancel…"

"Unless you're in handcuffs, you better plan on going. I'm not even sure Amy would forgive you if you *are* in handcuffs." Clara tipped her head, considering. "She might claim the best bunco night ever if you arrived in cuffs."

She chuckled alone.

"What?" she demanded. "You're completely in the clear and everybody there will know it. They can't possibly think you could have gotten past Marcus, not after how he reacted. *Twice.*"

Silence.

My heart dropped.

Teague O'Donnell had also recognized the demonstration didn't truly clear me.

"Marcus already knew Sheila was there at the dog park. You could say he was primed." He turned to me. "On a different day, if the wind were blowing the opposite way, could you get past without Marcus knowing?"

"I never have. I've also never taken meteorological measurements."

Irate, Clara said, "That's ridiculous."

He faced her. "In what way, Clara? Marcus had already greeted her today, before the test. He was primed."

"But … But you're making it sound like Sheila actually sneaked in there. Like she actually—when you know she couldn't have!"

He didn't relent. "The point is she *could* have. Quite easily, actually. Also, she could have come in from the other side."

I shot him a glance. Found him watching me, and looked away.

"What other side?" Clara demanded. "What do you mean?"

"He means I could have come from the woods and climbed the fence."

He shrugged. "It would've been easy. And I've heard you've talked about it."

"Maybe to avoid the mud at the entry," protested Clara, as if my reasoning made any difference.

"Both true. I have talked about climbing the fence and—as Clara says—it was in connection with trying to avoid the mud. You're missing several points, however. I was joking, but, okay, no way to prove that. Also, how would I have gotten Gracie over the fence? No way could I get over carrying a sixty-five-pound dog." Who would have been squirming and struggling to get free. But that wouldn't be as compelling an argument to skeptics who might hear of this discussion. Like, oh, say, Deputy Eckles via our corner deputy.

"You left her at home," Teague said instantly.

"I was at the post office and library just before getting to the dog park, with Gracie in my car. People must have seen her."

"You did it earlier—we don't know time of death—or you left her in your vehicle, parked somewhere nearby—"

"The sheriff's department parking lot no doubt," I inserted sarcastically.

"—walked in the back way, climbed the fence, killed him, went back the way you came, and—"

"If I could climb that fence, so could anyone else. Almost anyone else," I added, thinking of some of the dog park visitors.

He nodded, suddenly looking oddly cheerful. "True. Doesn't rule anybody out. In fact, it widens the pool of suspects."

"Suspects," repeated Clara. "You make it sound like Sheila is a— Like she…"

"Murdered Bob," I filled in.

"Sheila," she protested in an agonized whisper.

"Better to say it out loud than to let it fester."

"I wasn't saying that at all." His cheer remained. "Far too few facts in hand to say anything. I was simply pointing out the deputy's test was inadequate to clear Sheila."

Especially if I was right about the snow and Bob being killed much earlier.

The door opened and a deputy even younger than our corner-sitter said, "You next, Mr. O'Donnell."

CHAPTER ELEVEN

Either Deputy Eckles wasn't interviewing each of us or O'Donnell wasn't in there long, because Clara was called after only twenty minutes.

It was three times that before I was called.

At one point, I fished out paper and pen to make notes. Our friend in the corner said not to. He said it could alter my memory of events.

As if sitting in a stupor wouldn't.

Finally, I was called in. Gracie stayed with the observer deputy.

As the door closed, I'd swear I heard him say, "Okay, now we can play."

Deputy Eckles was in no mood for play.

Unless he considered going over the same material time after time a game.

I didn't.

"You're certain the dogs didn't disturb the body?"

"Not in my sight," I replied. Not for the first time.

I hadn't mentioned that I noticed their paws had made a mess of the ground around the body. If there'd been footprints there… But it was unlikely.

There'd certainly been no sign of footprints to or from the body except the dogs' and Clara's and mine. Not even Bob's.

That, added to the snow on Bob's jacket, said there'd been enough snow after he was killed to mask prints or marks of arrivals, as well as the murderer's departure.

I'd included the snow in my description of what I'd seen, but none of my thoughts about implications.

"But you couldn't see the dogs when they first encountered the body—isn't that your statement?"

"Yes."

"Yes, that's your statement?"

I cocked my head.

"Yes, Deputy Eckles, that is my statement." His lips parted. I straightened my head because he was just as annoying at an angle, and I spoke again before he could. "And, yes, that is what happened. There was also the flattened poop, as I said before."

"How long would you estimate the dogs were out of your sight?"

"They didn't step on it."

He grimaced. "How long were the dogs out of your sight?"

"That, too, is both my statement and what happened—I can't tell you precisely. Erring on the high side, certainly not more than three or four minutes."

"Mrs. Woodrow says the dogs did not disturb the body."

"She was in a better position to see what the dogs were doing before I was."

"Better—but that doesn't necessarily mean a good position, does it? It could be she was closer to the body, standing on the little rise, yet didn't see the body."

Was he trying to work out if Berrie might have gone into her usual small-dog enclosure, seen the body from there, and—A good question, actually. Could Las Vegas be seen from that small dog enclosure? I suspected it could. But I'd have to check.

When they re-opened the dog park. It was closed indefinitely, with police tape around the whole thing and down to the creek.

Surely, they'd check if Bob had been visible from the small dog enclosure…

But there I ground to a halt, trying to imagine why Berrie, his number one follower, wouldn't have immediately called 911.

Could she possibly have seen his body, then gone to the other enclosure, and proceeded with a session with the German shepherd and his owner?

"Deputy," I said with greater patience and calm than I'd known I possessed. "If Clara didn't see the body, we wouldn't be here."

Hensen, in the corner, coughed.

We returned to the tedium of giving my statement.

I must say it was a disappointment.

After decades of reading the phrase in murder mysteries, I'd thought it would offer an opportunity for dramatic flair for someone like me.

At last, he said he wanted me to come back the next day to sign a formal statement, but I could go for now.

I saw Berrie being led into Deputy Eckles' office as I retrieved Gracie from her playmate deputy.

Poor Berrie.

She looked dreadful.

Not only having lost her guru, but forced to be my oh-so-reluctant alibi.

Unless and until Deputy Eckles caught on to what O'Donnell had said. Presumably when the listening deputy reported to him.

CHAPTER TWELVE

I WENT TO bunco.

You might think, despite Clara's warning of Amy's retribution if I canceled, I should have stayed home with Gracie after her traumatic day.

Except she wasn't the least traumatized. Especially after all the petting, playing, and attention at the sheriff's department.

Also, there's this training approach I read about. The idea was to ease the dog's separation anxiety by giving her a favorite treat each time I left the house, so the dog associated departure with a goodie.

I'm not so sure Gracie had separation anxiety. But I had anxiety about her possibly having separation anxiety, considering her rescue background.

I tried the approach. She liked it. A lot.

After the first two times, Gracie had the equation down. Sheila leaves. *Yum.*

Now, whenever I showed signs of leaving, for example anything involving putting on normal shoes or gathering a purse and keys, Gracie immediately danced to the pantry where her much-loved teeth-cleaning treat was kept.

Last week, she'd poked me in the leg when my departure for my regular yoga class was behind her schedule. And it wasn't out of concern for my zen-like state.

Tonight, since bunco wasn't part of my routine, my leaving was pure bonus to Gracie.

Really, this training approach might have gone too far. I was getting a complex about my dog celebrating my departures.

Amy served what she called appetizers and most haute cuisine restaurants would call a main course. She was equally generous with wine and a hot buttered rum punch that could set off a Breathalyzer from a hundred feet.

Questions came at me fast and furious as we ate and throughout the first three rounds of bunco.

Before we started playing, Amy and Ruby, from the post office, offered some protection from the pushiest questioners. Once play started, I was on my own.

The points part of bunco is pretty simple. You roll three dice. You keep rolling as long as you're earning points. In Round One you get one point for each one that's rolled. If all three dice come up as ones, that's a bunco and earns twenty-one points. In Round Two, two becomes the point-getter. Any three-of-a-kind not matching the round number is a mini-bunco, worth five points.

We were settling into Round 4, with me rolling the dice, when my new partner said, "Such a shock about Bob Coble. I knew him in high school. Even then…" She looked around as if expecting someone to pick up on her words. No one did. "…he certainly threw himself into dogs. Had another of the same kind—what's it called—?"

"Gordon setter."

"—as before this one. Don't recall its name—"

"Trevalyn."

"—but he can recite that animal's whole family tree. You'd think he'd be more interested in his human family tree, what with being from an old North Bend County name. That dog was all he'd talk about at our last reunion."

After two rolls and three points, I passed on the dice.

The woman to my right said, "He always liked such things. Had to have his clothes just so. And his mama would work and work to get them that way for him."

My partner nodded, then zeroed in on me. "You and Clara Woodrow found Bob's body? I think I'd faint. But I heard you were very cool."

That almost sounded like criticism. "We both kept our heads to do what was necessary."

"I heard that when you and Clara arrived, Berrie was already there? And she was the only other one there until you found the body."

"There was another woman, too. Berrie was working with her dog."

"Ah, the woman scorned," murmured the woman to my right. Without looking up, she shouted, "Bunco!"

An echo came almost immediately from the head table. A bunco at the head table signaled the end of the round and a migration of players, melding a rugby scrum and musical chairs.

Each of the three tables was numbered, with one being the head table. Players across from each other were partners for that game, and won or lost as a team. Play continued until somebody at the head table reached twenty-one points. Winning players at the head table stayed there, while other winning players moved up a table. Head table losers dropped to the last table while all other losers stayed put.

That was confusing enough. Then they twisted it by having one of the players who stayed at a table move one chair, so partners—both staying and arriving—were broken up.

I watched, wistfully, as the woman who'd been to my right moved up to the head table. I'd love to hear what she meant about someone being a woman scorned. Berrie?

But she might have meant Augustine, the German shepherd owner. Could she have had a connection to Bob? She *had* opted for training with one of his vehements…

My partner from that super-short round moved to sit next to me.

To my satisfaction, she greeted the two newcomers to our table by asking one, "You used to live next door to Bob Coble when you were down in Blue Grass Estates, didn't you, Rosie?"

"Yes, for four long, long years."

The other women clicked their tongues sympathetically. "Terrible when you have bad neighbors," my ex-partner said.

"Much happier now, back here in Haines Tavern."

"And we're happy to have you," my former partner, now paired with "Rosie," said.

"I don't know what possessed us to ever think we'd like Blue Grass Estates, except Anthony got it in his head that belonging to that golf club would make him happy. It didn't. Did I tell you about when he tried to get up a foursome..."

My attention strayed.

There were nuances about living in North Bend County far outside my radar. But I had picked up enough in the first month to know factions centered around county seat Haines Tavern, the "big" town of Stringer, an upscale area centered around Blue Grass Estates, then rural areas south and west.

Clearly, I was surrounded here by Haines Tavern advocates.

When the golf club story wound down, I asked Rosie, "What made Bob Coble difficult to live next door to?"

"Neighborly love wasn't his style." For a moment, that appeared to be all the answer I'd get. She took a long drink from her wineglass, then looked at me from under her eyebrows. "He was always asking questions."

I took the jab and looked right back at her. "That doesn't sound so bad."

"He didn't stop there. I swear he looked into our windows. I also caught him looking at our mail more than once. He tried to say he was being helpful, bringing it in for us, but he was rifling through it. And I swear he tried to set his dog onto our cat. After I complained to the authorities about that dog barking, he started piling all its poop right next to our fence near the front walk, where our guests smelled it every time they came to our front door."

"How awful." My partner's sympathy sounded distracted. She appeared to be trying to discreetly fish for specific nuts in the bowl of mixed selection by her elbow. If she was looking for cashews, she was out of luck. I'd already fished those waters dry when I sat by the dish in an earlier round.

"He presented himself as such a stickler for rules. Telling everybody how they should run their lives and keep their yards. But did you know he wasn't supposed to be using that dog park? Every day he took that mutt there, he was breaking a rule."

"Well," demurred my partner from the previous round, a stylishly gray-haired woman now to my right, "it's for the whole county."

"Blue Grass Estates has its own dog park. That's the one he should have used. I long suspected he went to Torrid Avenue because it gave him a larger audience."

That was the most I heard about Bob.

As the evening wrapped up, I looked for the woman who'd used the woman scorned phrase, but she scooted out before I could catch her. I did find my partner from the fourth round.

"You said you went to school with Bob?"

"I did. Him and Dwight's mother, Kim." She shook her head. "Dwight turned out a whole lot better than her—or his father or any of that family. Had a cousin same age, real close as kids, but the cousin went one way and Dwight the other. Still, could have predicted Dwight and Bob wouldn't ever get along. Not the same types at all."

"Do you go to the dog park?"

"No, no. But I hear things, the way you do. My sister's husband's boss lives by Bob and the Yagoses have been here so long, lots of folks are intertwined with them one way or another."

"What about Bob? A nice guy, too?"

"Well, he was a particular kind of person, wasn't he? Excuse me, gotta go. My ride's leaving."

✧　✧　✧　✧

GRACIE SEEMED GLAD to see me return. Though she did eye the door several times, like if I left again maybe she'd get another treat.

Clara had left a phone message, including instructions to call her back tonight no matter the time. I obeyed.

"What did you hear at bunco?" she demanded immediately.

I took off my right shoe and rubbed my instep. "I probably said more than I heard."

But I gave her a few highlights.

"Darn. I wish I knew who you'd talked to. We could question them again and—"

"Question them?"

"—get more details. I called Dwight's phone, but his mailbox is full. I know the Yagoses some, but Dwight was way ahead of me in school, much less Bob. I wonder if my older sister knows them. If only I hadn't spent so much time avoiding them—"

"You avoided them for the very sensible reason that being around either one pitched you into the middle of their rivalry."

"Well, yeah, but now the background might help us with detecting."

"Whoa. Detecting?" Okay, I'd entertained the thought myself, but...

"Of course. We were *there*. It's ... It's almost like a *duty*."

"We did our duty by not messing up the scene, calling the authorities, and telling them the truth. Now, it's the sheriff's department's duty."

Her sigh might have blown me over if it hadn't come through a phone. "You've probably lived a much more exciting life than I have—"

"High school teacher, remember? English."

"Still, with your inheritance and living in New York..."

"Upstate. Not that different from here, except colder."

"Still, you've had more experience. You know things from reading important books I've never read, on top of all those mysteries I saw at your house. We could find out stuff. It's not like I wanted Bob murdered and if I could bring him back by not being interested I'd do it in a heartbeat, but this is probably my only chance ever—"

"Clara, I don't think we should try to get involved." I understood her interest. Part of me was itching ... "Not to mention Deputy Eckles would not appreciate it."

"Oh, him, He wouldn't appreciate us getting involved because he's suspicious of you. As for being involved, you *are* involved. As a suspect."

That's what worried me. The last thing I needed was being accused of murder.

I suppose that was the last thing most people needed.

But in my case it was amplified because attention might reveal my connection to *Abandon All*, which would mean a mess for me and Aunt Kit.

Then there was the flip side.

I *had* picked up a lot on research trips and training with Aunt Kit.

She'd written mysteries under various names for much of her writing career and continued to write them now. Kit drew me into brainstorming them and to my surprise I had a knack for what the sleuth could or should look into next.

To my even greater surprise, what I'd learned had benefits a few months ago, on a cruise ship, when knowing my fellow passengers and having access to information not shared with officials helped find a murderer.

After that, I'd thought I wouldn't mind grappling with another mystery. I rather enjoyed the sleuthing.

I hadn't been thinking about the potential attention.

But a tactic I'd used on the cruise could help again. As long as I funneled my brilliant insights—please, let there be brilliant insights— through Clara, she would be in the spotlight and I could stand in her shadow.

"You're right."

"Yippee! What do we do first?"

CHAPTER THIRTEEN

"LET'S START WITH what you know about him."

"Not much. I know Dwight's single. He worked for one of the delivery services, but quit when he started caring for his grandmother full-time. He never went back when she moved into the senior home. He and his grandmother are real close. His parents lived with her while he was growing up. Freeloading most folks say, because his grandmother has money. They finally got their own house when he was in his teens. But he moved back in with her when he was, oh, maybe in his late twenties. He was real serious about a girl and his parents didn't approve, but his grandmother took him in."

The guy had to be around forty. He couldn't live on his own? Have his own apartment maybe? Of course, who was I to talk, having lived with my great-aunt for the past decade-and-a-half?

"How does Dwight have time to come to the dog park during the middle of the day?"

I hadn't wondered about that until Teague asked me. There were enough of us who came during the middle of the day that it almost seemed normal.

"How'd he get into dogs?"

"I think his grandmother taught him about them. But he said his ideas about dogs came mostly from his own experiences."

"Anything else?"

"He's allergic to figs. His face got all puffy and turned red when there was fig in a fruit bread he ate. He's an excellent Scrabble player. A fan of the Kentucky Wildcats, but he wasn't one of those really obnoxious kinds, because we got along and I'm a Louisville fan. And his favorite cookie is chocolate chip."

I stared at the phone. "You don't know his socks size?"

"Oh, I'd say large."

"Clara, you are a wonder."

"Will you tell that to my husband?"

"Absolutely. But how do you know all this?"

"We were in a support group together for a while offered through the County Extension. For caretakers. I was caring for Mother Woodrow then. Dwight came while he was caring for his grandmother at home. Once she went to a place for seniors—she was having trouble with memory, could've burned down the house a couple times from things left on the stove—he didn't seem to have the same need. Stopped coming."

"Is she still alive?"

"Oh yes. I'm sure I would have heard if she passed away."

"Do you know where she lives?"

"Yes. Kentucky Manor, the senior residence off Zig-Zag."

She said that as if it would mean something to me. "Clara? Do you know the family well enough for us to go visit her?"

"Maybe. If you think it's a good idea?"

"Well, let's see what happens after the deputies question Dwight, if they haven't already. After Berrie's outburst, I bet that was their first stop."

"See, you know all this stuff I never would."

"Uh-huh. But when I asked what you knew about him, I actually meant Bob Coble. It's one of the tenets—" I almost said of writing mysteries. But that edged close to Aunt Kit and her history, which was a path I did not want to go down. "—in all the mysteries I read that knowing about the victim can tell a lot about what happened and why."

"You know so much about these things," she said admiringly.

"I don't, only what I've read in—"

"I know. All the books you read to be an English teacher. I need to read more."

I wished I could tell her I'd learned more—far more—about victimology from hanging around Aunt Kit, watching her process, and reading her books and those she recommended, than from the English classes that might have, in an alternate universe, sent me into a classroom as an English teacher.

"One of the women at bunco said Bob came from an old county family."

"I guess. There's a Coble Park and a Coble Road."

"Married?"

"No. Possibly gay, though I've never heard anybody say so."

"No gossip?"

"It's kind of old-fashioned to gossip about if someone's gay or not."

I'd hope so, but it wasn't always so.

Gracie got up from her comfortable snooze on her dog bed, came to the side of my upholstered chair, and stared directly at me, wagging her tail. It was an invitation—possibly a command—to admire her and more importantly pet her.

When I complied, her ears tucked close to her head in bliss.

For once, she sat still for a good, long pet. Nothing like a murder and finding a dead body and all that attention at the sheriff's department to make a dog ready to receive affection. Or was she giving it?

"He has a house in Blue Grass Estates. Bob worked for a company in Cincinnati for years, then got a buy-out offer. Early retirement, I guess. A real good package. That's when he started coming to the dog park from what I hear."

Clara released a short, sharp breath.

"I'll say it right out, Sheila. He could be mean, real mean."

"To dogs? I never saw—"

"Oh, no. Not dogs. Never, even with the ones he thought were too rough or too ... *common* to be around Trevalyn. But if you'd told me someone I knew was going to be murdered, I'd've said Bob. And if you'd told me someone I knew was going to *commit* murder ... Well, I'd've said Bob for that, too. Though I probably wouldn't have said anything because I wouldn't have believed it. I know what I said about

Bob, but I wouldn't have really believed it. Not Bob a murder victim. Not Dwight a murder suspect."

I agreed.

Watching those two men argue over the past month gave me the feeling the same conversation had been going on for ages and would go on forever.

"But there *was* a murder," she added, sounding lost. Then she perked up. "It's a good thing you're here to help."

"I'm sure Deputy Eckles will be thrilled."

"He doesn't understand how the dog park operates," Clara said. "Once he gets more background, he'll understand that what might look suspicious to him isn't suspicious at all."

"Speaking of suspicious, what did you think of how Teague O'Donnell reacted?"

"*Teague?* You're not thinking he…? But he's so nice. I mean I suppose a murderer can be nice but he never even talked with Bob or Dwight that I know of, did he?"

"Since we're nearly always at the dog park together, if you didn't see him talking to one or both of them, I didn't either. But there was something about his reactions today that made me wonder. Did you notice, he essentially closed off the entrance to the parking lot to regular folks?"

"I thought that was smart."

Maybe I was reading too much into Teague's actions. He could be one of those people who reacted well under pressure. I don't fall apart either. At least not on the outside. Inside I might have some crumbling going on, but I don't let it out.

"Tell me about Berrie and her Boston terriers."

"Berrie? You can't possibly think Berrie is the killer."

"I'm curious about her. Just curious."

"Besides, how could she kill somebody with those dogs barking all around her? I can't imagine them being quiet if there was any activity."

"I don't know, but…"

"You're right, you're right. I want to investigate, then when you start doing it, I shoot down your questions. I'm sorry, Sheila. Real sorry."

"It's okay."

Gracie stood up, staring intently again.

"Good. Berrie. She's been coming to the dog park longer than I have. When I started coming, she had three Boston terriers already. She's adopted at least one more. Plus, she does rescue. So, yeah, she's a pain, but…" Clara's tone said that anyone who did dog rescue could not possibly be a bad person.

That might pose a problem, since everyone I knew of who'd had contact with Bob Coble was good to dogs. If we had to go beyond the dog park to look into Bob's life, we'd be starting from scratch.

"Clara—?" Gracie barked. Short, commanding, precise. I knew that bark. To ignore it was to face unpleasant consequences. "I've gotta go. Gracie has to go out. We'll talk tomorrow."

CHAPTER FOURTEEN

I TOOK THE calculated risk of calling Kit the next morning before Teague O'Donnell was scheduled to arrive … assuming he didn't go by contractors' time, which had no relation to the clock or calendar.

I'd considered calling Kit last night, to tell her about the murder. After bunco and talking with Clara, though, it was too late.

For me. Not for Kit.

My great-aunt kept the hours of a teenage gamer.

Which is why calling her now was a risk.

"*What?*" she answered.

"It's Sheila, Kit. Nothing's wrong with anybody in the family." I had to get that in fast, because she'd assume the worst would be the only reason I'd call at this hour.

The silence said her morning brain was processing. "Why are you whispering?"

"A workman's supposed to come soon and I don't want him to hear."

"Hear what? He'd have to have the world's best hearing, especially from outside your house. Not to mention you haven't said anything yet. You're acting like there's something big, like—*No.*"

I suspected I was going to get that same response—the disbelieving no—if my parents found out. But the tenor of the word and the emotion behind it would be totally different.

I kept going.

"I've told you, about taking my dog, Gracie, to the dog park, right? Well, when we got there—with Clara. I've told you about her too, right?—and her dog, LuLu. Well, we were almost the first ones at the dog park, which doesn't happen often because—"

"*Murder.* You're involved in another *murder.*"

"How can you possibly know that?"

"I can't imagine anything else you would be this reluctant to tell me. All those years of us living together and not a single murder came across our path. Now you've had two—*two*—in just a few months. If you had a magnetism for murders, why did you wait until now to display it?"

"It's not like this is something *I'm* doing, Kit," I protested. "I have nothing to do with these murders happening."

"So you say."

I groaned. "You sound like the North Bend County deputy who kept questioning me yesterday."

"Yesterday! This murder happened yesterday and you waited until now to call me?"

"Questioned by deputies. Did you hear that part? Over and over and over. At the scene and then at the sheriff's department. I swear, Kit, they consider me a suspect. Can we focus on that?"

"I'll console myself that you called me about this before your mother."

"How do you know I haven't called Mom?"

"Because she would have already been on the phone to me, terri-fied that you are tied up in a murder case." Tied up. The phrase brought an image ... that leash around Bob's neck. "Okay, let's back up. You and your dog were at the dog park yesterday."

"Yes. And my friend, Clara, and I found the body. Well, our dogs did, but we were the first humans on the scene."

I heard a rustle, like someone sitting up in bed. Kit said briskly, "Tell me precisely what happened."

I did. Straight through the interrogations to going to bunco last night and quickly filling her in on the little bit I learned there.

She grumbled something about whether phones worked after ten p.m. in Kentucky, but I figured I got off light.

I could have called her after talking with Clara. My night owl great-aunt certainly would have been awake. But I'd been exhausted. Too much had happened, too much was in my head to present it even half coherently.

And I must have been at least half coherent now or I would have heard about it from Kit.

"Give me the character sketch."

I knew she meant the victim. "White male, near retirement age. Apparently financially comfortable. Very emotionally invested in his dog to the—"

"And you're not?" She snorted. "All I hear is Gracie this and Gracie that."

"—point that he doesn't recognize reality."

"Uh-huh."

"I love Gracie, but I don't think that not only is she the best-trained dog ever, but that I am the best trainer, following the convoluted specious argument that I must be because she's the best dog ever and I trained her."

This snort acknowledged I might have a point.

"He had a dispute with former neighbors. They called animal control on Trevalyn—that's his dog."

"What for?"

"I don't know for sure. I'd guess probably noise." Rosie hadn't made it clear, and I might be sensitized to the noise issue, because Gracie tended to bark. I brought her inside the second she started, though. So someone living in my house could complain, but not the neighbors.

"Don't guess. Find out. Neighbor disputes stir a lot of emotions and can get nasty."

"Fine, fine. We'll check it out."

"We?"

"Clara and I."

I tried for casual. Kit's reaction said I didn't succeed. "Clara, the woman from the dog park?" She didn't wait for confirmation, she already knew the answer. "Why are you involving someone else? Petronella was one thing, but someone outside the family…"

Petronella, a relative only according to the way my great-aunt figured family, had been with me on the cruise. My brothers described her as several sandwiches short of a picnic. Which could be annoying, but she had turned out to be oddly helpful in sorting out the murder onboard.

"Clara knows the area. The history, the ins and outs, the people. Besides, I told you how talking things over with Petronella helped me figure out what happened on the cruise last fall."

An abbreviated *huh* scoffed at my statement.

"It did," I argued with that *huh*. "And Petronella started standing up for herself more by the end of that trip."

"The trip did Petronella good. Still needs something resembling a backbone, but she's definitely better. That doesn't change that I know what you did, Sheila. You gave her all the credit for figuring out what happened in that murder case. Petronella didn't—wouldn't—have a clue. Literally. And I suspect I know why you did it. Didn't want the author of *Abandon All* in the spotlight."

"It would be awkward."

"It would." She sounded thoughtful. That could be dangerous. "You're planning on putting this Clara in the same role as Petronella? You solve it, then give her the credit, so you can melt into the background?"

My chuckle was about as long as her abbreviated *huh*. "You're giving me way too much credit for being as Machiavellian as you are. But I might have met someone who is."

I told her about Teague O'Donnell and what he said about the demonstration of Marcus' reaction to me.

"He said all that with a deputy there in the room?" Kit asked at the end.

"I know. The jerk."

"He did you a favor."

"What?" That was reflexive. My brain was already grappling with it. "Okay, I can see he didn't actually hurt me by pointing out the test was flawed, because anyone would eventually see the same flaws, though I'm not entirely convinced Eckles—But Deputy Hensen would have spotted the flaws without O'Donnell's help soon if he hadn't already. But then O'Donnell went ahead and said how I could have done it another way by coming over the outside fence and that—Oh."

"Finally. I was beginning to wonder where your brain had gone to."

"He pointed out the field of suspects could be wide open. Not limited to the people at the dog park yesterday morning."

"Precisely. Now, sounds to me like you have a lot to find out. You've barely scratched the surface. And you didn't know this victim well, losing your opportunity to get an inside track."

"If I'd known he was going to be murdered," I said dryly, "I would not have been so careless."

"Maybe you'll be better next time."

"*Next time?*"

But Kit was going on, "You need a lot more background information on this Bob Coble. All you seem to know about him concerns dogs. Find out about his life. His personal life. His work life. His love life. All of it. You need to know all of it. Anything you can find out about him."

"Isn't the first question if he had any enemies? He did. Dwight from the dog park I told you about."

"Are you saying dog park disputes are a motive for murder?"

"The passions do run high," I muttered. It had been a lot funnier when Clara, Teague, and I joked about it two days ago. "Besides, there have been murders about making cheerleading squads and even less. Why not dog training? What it comes down to is their position in the pack. At least that's how they both seemed to see it. And they both wanted to be the leader, not noticing or caring that most of us didn't follow either one of them."

"Okay, that's an angle, but don't let it be your only angle. There are too many other possible aspects. You don't want to trip during a rush to judgment."

"I wouldn't mind Deputy Eckles tripping, since he appears to be rushing to a judgment about me."

"Idiot." For some reason, that made me feel better. "But that security chief on the ship considered you the prime suspect and that turned out fine."

"I've thought about that. I wouldn't be surprised if he'd let me think he thought that to motivate me to snoop. Besides, I was a lot more optimistic about his ability to come to the right conclusion in the end than I am about Deputy Eckles."

"Don't sell law enforcement short."

"I have as much respect for law enforcement as you do, Kit, but with this guy, it's like we found this body to annoy him and he's looking for the fastest, easiest way to deal with it."

She clicked her tongue. "I've seen a few like that—in law enforcement and everywhere else. Now, send me the full names and addresses and any other background information of everyone you can think of who's involved. I'll see what I can find out. At least this time we have normal communication, instead of you being out in the middle of the ocean somewhere."

"Hey, who sent me out in the middle of the ocean somewhere? Wasn't my idea."

"It was for your own good."

I couldn't argue with that. At least I wouldn't.

I promised to email her all the official information I had on Bob Coble. Some from the dog park, some from a quick Google search of my own, some from an article in this morning's paper.

I heard a vehicle pulling up outside and said I had to go.

"Your workman?"

"Maybe."

She snort-laughed. "Not your workman. But I won't ask what you're up to. I'm going back to sleep now so I can think about your problem and get some writing done later."

CHAPTER FIFTEEN

"**...AND WHAT ABOUT** that woman saying something about Berrie being a woman scorned?" I said to Clara as I opened the door fifteen minutes later to Teague and Murphy.

His brows rose when LuLu bounded toward the door with Gracie in pursuit. "Dog sitting?"

He'd unhooked Murphy's leash as he asked the question and now his dog scooted past us to the joy of the two others.

All three careened through the dining room, into the small kitchen, found the connecting back hall that brought them around to the relative openness of the living room, allowing them to gather steam before plowing into Teague and me, still standing at the door.

"Woohoo," Clara exclaimed from her safe seat in the living room. "That must have been an express train."

Now Teague's eyebrows really popped up. I shrugged. "I figured it would be more fun for the dogs with all of us here, since the park's closed."

That's what I'd told Clara, too, when I'd invited her to come over a quarter of an hour before Teague was supposed to arrive.

"Yeah, they'll enjoy me taking measurements of where you want these shelves and discussing design decisions."

"Design?" Clara repeated. "What we need to talk about is the murder. Sheila found out all sorts of interesting things last night at bunco."

Teague's eyebrows should give up and stay in the raised position or the muscles doing the hiking and dropping were going to get worn out.

"A little background information," I said.

"Is that the same as gossip?"

"Close," Clara said. "But with a purpose. It's like on those TV shows, you've got to find out about the victim. We're trying to remember everything we know, but after all that time spent avoiding Bob—Dwight, too—we don't know as much as you might think."

"I wouldn't expect to know much about him at all, considering I've only been here a month. Gracie, no! Sit!"

The dogs' second go-around, which left rugs flung wild behind them, had brought them back into the living room where Teague and I stood talking to Clara. Gracie apparently felt she had been losing ground so she took a shortcut by jumping onto, then over the back of an upholstered chair. I had to give her credit, it put her right at Murphy's shoulder. Perfect positioning for a little friendly neck chewing to herd him toward the stairs.

With a vision of the open boxes spread in the upstairs hallway, I leapt to the bottom stair and spread-eagled across the opening to block the dogs.

The others called to their dogs and, more effectively, grabbed their collars.

Belatedly, Gracie sat, now that there was no one to chase.

"Nice place," Teague said.

It was. Both years ago and before this dog invasion.

It had a square floor plan, with the dining room to the left of the front door, connecting to the kitchen behind it, which connected to the living room with a classic brick fireplace, then back to the compact foyer, with the stairs heading up from there. A powder room was tucked in back by the stairs down to the basement. A screened-in porch started off the living room, then wrapped around the back.

Upstairs, three bedrooms echoed the rooms downstairs, with the master bedroom, with its own compact bathroom, plus the main bath serving the other two bedrooms. The most compact of those rooms now served as my office.

Have you noticed *compact* as a theme of this house?

"That must have been some inheritance." He looked around while bent over holding Murphy's collar.

"Real estate isn't that expensive around here."

"Not Chicago prices, but more than a substitute teacher could swing without investments."

That jangled something in my brain. "But you're supporting yourself by subbing?"

"Reminds me what you said the day we met, Teague," Clara said with a bright smile before he could answer. "About how teaching is investing in the next generation, remember?"

And darned if Mr. Unflappable didn't look irked. "That's—"

"Helping kids who need it the most." She turned her earnest face toward me. "He works with at-risk students."

"That's very admirable." I was trying to figure out why he would have preferred Clara hadn't revealed that.

"No more than any other teacher in the building."

"And I bet Sheila got a deal on this place, because it's going to take a lot to fix it up," Clara said cheerfully. "A money pit. It's a good thing that inheritance was generous."

"I was fortunate. The payoff for having the old-fashioned name Sheila. That's why she chose me. Distant relative. Let's go upstairs and see the office and closet where I want the shelves."

"Good idea."

"No." Clara objected. "There's so much more for Sheila to tell us about last night."

"What makes you think I have any more to say?" I tried to give her the signal to drop it.

Something went wrong between my signal-sending and her receiving.

"I can tell by your face. You wouldn't have invited me over this morning unless you had more news than just that little bit. Oh." Her gaze shifted from me to Teague and back. "Or would you?"

This time Teague kept his eyebrows in order but sputtered out a chuckle.

What was I supposed to say after that? "Let's do the measuring first and then we can have coffee."

That gave Teague an out, which I fully expected him to take.

"Sounds good. We can talk then," he said. "Show me the way and I'll get the measurements."

Which took longer than it needed to since we were accompanied by all three dogs and Clara.

To get us all in the small room, Teague moved behind the desk, where I'd left my computer on.

He looked at the screen, but didn't react.

The screensaver might have covered my searches to confirm what I'd thought about the snow on Bob's jacket. In a low area protected from sun, it could have fallen at night and still been there in the morning. Or maybe he didn't recognize the significance, since he hadn't seen Bob's body yesterday.

"You've got a lot of books." His gaze lingered on the mysteries and a selection of research books. Was I missing books every high school teacher would have? "Somehow, you don't strike me as a teacher."

"That was my secret weapon in the classroom. I snuck up on them."

"Snuck?"

Darn. Aunt Kit would gloat if that error got me in trouble. "Colloquial for sneaked, of course."

He smiled.

That smile … I wasn't sure I liked that smile. It reminded me of the smile of an interviewer accepting that you'd successfully fended off *this* intrusion into your personal life, but planning another one soon.

"That's the reason for more shelves, even though I left a lot of books behind when I moved. Traveling light." Hoped that covered any gaps in my collection.

He not only appeared unaffected by my coolness, but I could swear his mouth twitched.

"You can't see anything from back there," I said. If the damage hadn't already been done, no sense leaving him by the computer. "The shelves will be over here. What I thought…"

He had opinions, including good ideas I hadn't thought about. The dogs had no opinions, but that didn't stop them from wanting to be in the middle of whatever we were doing. In addition, LuLu took exception to the sound of Teague's metal tape measure extending and retracting. I couldn't imagine this was the easiest quote he'd ever given.

Still, I was impressed. For a high school teacher, he certainly seemed to know his carpentry. He understood what I was aiming for when I didn't feel I had been particularly articulate. He gave a bid in the ballpark of the other two contractors—out of the seven I started with—who'd gotten that far. And with a tighter timeline.

"What happens to the timeline if you get called in to teach?"

Clara slid a disapproving look at me.

"I could still work on this project nights and weekends and it shouldn't take all that much longer. Say, add three days if you want me to do the painting."

"I do. Give me something in writing and let me think about it."

"Oh, for heaven's sakes, you're going to hire him. He's more reasonable than the other quotes you got and he will actually do the work. Especially," Clara said cheerfully, "because we could track him down at the dog park and make his life miserable if he doesn't."

"Strong motivation," Teague murmured.

"Nothing like obliterating my bargaining power, Clara."

"I'll have tea," she responded. "While you tell us *all* about last night."

CHAPTER SIXTEEN

I DID TELL them all about bunco.

But only after an interlude with the dogs outside careening around the yard and throwing up divots of what had once been grass with their sharpest turns, followed by coffee, tea, and a plate of the last few cookies left over from my baking and shipping.

Teague praised the cookies, but Clara cut him off.

"I told that deputy—actually deputies—yesterday that they shouldn't entirely dismiss what Berrie said and they should look into the conflict between the Dwights and Bobs. I told them about the bad feelings and the arguments. Including what happened the day before yesterday."

"That doesn't seem like much of a motive for murder," Teague said.

"You only saw them that once and Sheila hasn't seen much more. A small slice of all the days and months and years of it brewing and simmering and building. Besides, there's nobody else."

Teague flickered a look toward me.

Great.

I'd been hoping it was my paranoia.

"You can't think it was Sheila," Clara said with more loyalty than tact.

"I'm not thinking anything. But the deputies certainly seemed interested in Sheila's actions and timeline."

"They're picking on her because she's a newcomer and—"

Interesting they didn't focus on O'Donnell then.

"—that's even more reason we have to show them the truth. Why aren't they out looking for Dwight?"

"I'm sure they are."

His assurance clearly did not cut it with Clara. Me, either, for that matter.

Clara, apparently looking for the silver lining, said, "It's amazing people get along as well as they do."

"At the dog park?" Amusement tinged his disbelief. "We're back to passions at the dog park?"

"Less fervent, more murderous," I murmured.

That sobered him. "There's no guarantee that it had anything to do with dogs in general or the dog park in particular."

"Hmmm."

"What does that mean?"

"It means a dog trainer being strangled with a dog leash at a dog park makes me think it might just have something to do with the world of dogs."

He ignored that, as men tend to do when they've been out-thought. "The dog park at night is mighty convenient for a murderer—dark, isolated, unobserved."

"And prone to unexpected encounters with poop."

Clara and I exchanged a look.

"What?" Teague asked.

"We told the deputies," Clara said. "There was an old poop smooshed wide, like someone had stepped—and slipped—on it. It wasn't on Bob's shoes."

The humor edged back in to Teague's eyes. "You want the sheriff's department to do a poop lineup of everyone's shoes in the county."

I nodded slowly. "A sort of twisted Cinderella hunt. But the thing is, even if they found the shoe with the poop, the wearer could easily explain it—as long as he or she is a dog park regular. They should have done it right away. Too late now."

"Couldn't they do DNA and—"

Teague punctured her hopes. "Does North Bend County's sheriff's department have a lot of money to spare for dog poop DNA?

Especially since it could have come from a different encounter with that dog's poop."

"Good point," I conceded. "Though it could have pointed to a few people."

Clara sighed. "What I don't understand is what Bob was doing there at the dog park without Trevalyn and how did he get in? I cannot imagine him climbing over the fence, although I suppose he must have."

Teague looked from her to me. "If he was the first one there in the morning…"

"Oh, no, didn't you know? His body was there overnight. Or at least some of the night."

"What?" He faced me. "Did you know this?"

"Of course she did," Clara said before I could answer. "She saw the snow, too."

So much for keeping that to myself.

"What snow?"

"The snow on Bob's body. So he must have been killed and left there from sometime during the night. But I don't understand why he would have gone there at night. Who he would have met there. Without Trevalyn, with that leash—lead."

Teague leaned back in his chair. "Do you realize…? This thing is totally open. Does *anybody* have an alibi?"

"Clara does. Her husband, Ned. And I suppose a number of other couples."

She looked at him, then me. "What do you mean?"

Teague answered. "If Bob Coble was killed during the night, it means just about anybody could have killed him."

"No, it doesn't. Because it would have to be somebody who could get Bob to go there at that time of night and there aren't many people who could do that."

"Good point, Clara. Teague's right that as far as opportunity it opens the field, but you are right that realistically it narrows it. But it still leaves a lot of possible whos. Let's look at it from the what—what could lure Bob Coble to the closed dog park during the night, when he'd have to climb the fence?"

"Money," Teague proposed.

"No." Clara and I were unanimous.

Silence descended. I drank more tea. Clara stirred hers. Teague ate a cookie. Then a second. Then a third.

Clara and I looked up simultaneously.

"A dog," she said.

"A chance to show off," I said.

"A chance to show off about a dog, would that do it?" Teague asked.

"Absolutely."

"But doesn't that leave the field as open as before? Everybody we've considered has a dog, right?"

Clara deflated. "Yeah."

Except Ruby, I mentally added, though she used to.

"And that leaves the other question unanswered." They both turned to me. "Why was Bob strangled with Trevalyn's leash?

CHAPTER SEVENTEEN

DEPUTY **E**CKLES **SQUASHED** all flair in my statement. Or style. Or voice. I made a stand on grammar. He didn't appreciate it, but the man wanted me to affix my signature to a paper that included "It was a shock for Clara and I."

Me, Deputy Eckles. For Clara and *me*.

When I'd arrived, I'd given my name, and said I was here to sign a statement, I was told Deputy Eckles would see me.

I suspected he regretted that now.

First, I'd read the statement carefully, finding several typos in addition to the egregious *me*. Then I'd insisted they be fixed.

While we waited for the revised edition's turn to emerge from an overworked printer, the deputy initiated this latest round of repetitive questioning.

"I meant," he picked up, "Clara Woodrow might not have seen one or the other dogs have contact with the body."

"What did you find that makes you think one of the dogs touched the body?"

"Why do you ask that, Ms. Mackey?" His deadpan screamed suspicion.

I leaned my elbows on the table and looked directly at him. "Deputy Eckles, surely no one you question can be as stupid as I would have to be to not draw that conclusion."

"Oh, he deals with some pretty stupid ones," Hensen muttered.

"Hensen," Eckles snapped.

There was a moment of tense silence, which I eased by leaning back once more. "So, you're not going to tell me what you found?"

"No."

I barely waited for that—no sense letting him realize he'd at least tacitly confirmed my supposition. "Well, I'm sorry I can't help you any with that, but I can tell you neither dog touched the body from the time I first caught sight of it. And if Clara says they didn't before I could see the body, then you have your answer."

He grunted. Not happily.

The statement was delivered at that moment. I read it over again. Sighed over the plodding prose, signed, and stood.

"I'm sorry I can't help."

"Are you?"

That struck me as downright rude. I frowned.

Eckles went on. "I hear you and the victim never got along."

I chuckled. "I hear Berrie Vittlow's voice in that statement."

"Why would she say it if it weren't true?"

"Because I don't adhere to her views on dog-training. That's the same reason I mostly steered clear of Bob Coble in the four weeks I've been going to the dog park." He didn't appear to heed my emphasis on how short a time I'd known Bob. "I didn't care for him—tedious and portentous."

"Pretentious?"

"Portentous," I repeated. "Given to making each and every utterance sound as if it were foretelling the future."

"So, you didn't like him."

"I steered clear of him. Not the same thing."

"Over dog training." He practically sneered at that.

"Yes."

"This is a murder investigation. That's far more important than a feud over dog training."

Did that mean he was ignoring Dwight Yagos?

"I had no feud with Bob. I simply avoided him when possible, which all happened before he was murdered."

"Over dog training?" He dripped disbelief.

"Ah, Deputy. You don't know dog lovers."

"I do after this," he grumbled.

I'D LEFT THE hardware store, which, after the Torrid Avenue Dog Park, seemed to be where I spent most of my time.

If you have never owned a house, you would be astonished to know how many trips to the hardware store are required each week.

At least I'm astonished by it.

Another gap in my life experience.

I helped organize some of the upkeep on the Manhattan brownstone, but more was handled by Aunt Kit or the housekeeper. Plus, it had already been restored when we moved in. My house here was in the state TV real estate shows blithely call "before" for the nanosecond shot before they dwell lovingly on the "after."

This trip had been for faucet washers, since the one I removed during explorations to explain a persistent drip from the first floor powder room sink had disintegrated, partly in my hand, partly in the screwed off drain gizmo. That's the technical name for it.

Washers in my pocket, I moved on to the post office.

I walked into a firestorm.

Berrie Vittlow screamed, red-faced. Ruby, behind the counter, held onto its edge. Amy stood rigidly against the wall next to the door. The newspaper reader in the corner looked as if he'd been blasted back by an explosion.

"You killed him. You all killed him. All he wanted to do was help you and show people the best way with their dogs and everything else. And you all rejected him. You killed his soul."

"Oh, come on, Berrie," Amy said. "We're all sorry Bob is dead, but that doesn't blind us to—"

"You aren't. You aren't sorry. You wanted him dead. You could be the one who killed him."

"Now, Berrie, we know you're upset, but you can't be saying things like that," Ruby started.

"You! You were among the worst of all."

That surprised me. Ruby had been a bit tart with Bob when he got out of sorts about Gracie being in the post office, but their discussion hadn't struck me as being anywhere close to as acrimonious as the ones at the dog park. I'd figured people didn't get as worked up about the post office as they did about their dogs.

Berrie's comment now opened my thinking. The expression going postal hadn't come from nowhere. Though in this instance Bob had seemed a far more likely candidate than Ruby. Except his candidacy carried the distinct drawback that he was dead.

"You wanted him dead when all he wanted was the rules followed," Berrie accused.

I've taken care of Bob Coble.

Ruby had said that. But surely…

"The rules followed?" Amy said. "That's hogwash. He used rules as a weapon. Look at the things he said about Ruby. The nasty—"

"That's a vicious, vicious lie. As bad as those other lies you've told about him. All of you." She swung around at Amy. "All the lies you told, he was so much better with dogs, with everything than the rest of you can ever hope to be."

Ruby tried again. "Berrie, I know you are upset. I truly am sorry for your loss. But you cannot be saying things like that, especially not in my post office. You need to get ahold of yourself. Nobody is saying Bob Coble was all bad. He was as good as he could be to dogs and that says something important about a man. And that's coming from me, threatened more than once by one of his lawsuits. Heaven knows I wasn't the only one. The man would threaten to sue you as soon as look at you. Me, his neighbors, the people at the dog park, about every business in town and a lot of them beyond. He threatened to sue people the way some people go to church—once a day and twice on Sunday."

"He had every right to sue you. You and all the others breaking the rules. But he showed great restraint and generosity by not filing all the suits he could have. That's the kind of man he was."

A woman about my age, perhaps a few years younger, and wearing a cloche hat with a lot more style then I ever managed, pushed open the door from the square, and froze.

"What about the lawsuit he threatened to file against you, Berrie? After all the years you've been friends, after all the support you've given him?"

Whoa. Bob threatened to sue Berrie? What on earth was that about?

The woman at the door pivoted and walked out. There probably wasn't room for her in here, anyway.

I suppose some people respond that way to conflict. Aunt Kit had taught me conflict was the grist for fiction's mill. It can be a lot more subtle than these harsh words and cross-accusations, but these work fine, too.

Berrie's face turned darker red. She turned, blundered into a display of mailing boxes, then rocked the other way, before grabbing the door, which hadn't closed quite all the way yet, and followed the cloche-hatted woman.

Not wanting the others to get their equilibrium—and discretion—locked into place, I asked, "What was Berrie talking about, when she said lies were told about Bob?"

I was being tactful, leaving out the part about Ruby and Amy being among the liars according to Berrie.

Ruby and Amy looked at each other. As fast as I'd asked my question, it was already too late. I wasn't going to get an answer.

"It's all ancient, ancient history," Ruby said. "Now, what can I do for you, Amy? Let's get you taken care of so you can get back to work at the library."

CHAPTER EIGHTEEN

EVEN WITHOUT CALLER ID, I'd have known it was Clara by the way she barely waited for my hello.

"Sheila, did you sign your statement? Did Deputy Eckles tell you anything? Did you learn anything at the sheriff's department? I didn't pick up anything while I was there. I guess I got there right after you'd left because the clerk told Eckles on the phone that he had *another one*. I went by the dog park first. It's still all wrapped in police tape. The whole thing and there's a sign that it's closed until further notice. I wonder how long they can keep it closed. LuLu is going to go nuts if she can't run off some of her energy."

It sounded like LuLu wasn't the only one.

"Anything about Dwight?"

"No, nobody's seen him and no activity at his house. My gran used to live near there and I talked to her old neighbor."

I told Clara about the scene in the post office.

"Oh, the lawsuits. That's good. That's really good. I've heard Donna say something about Bob threatening people with lawsuits. So, what do we do next?"

"I'm going to eat dinner then take Gracie to her class at Zepke's." I liked that the local pet store skipped any cutesy names and used the owner's name. It looked more dignified on my credit card statement when I bought an outrageous volume of food, treats, furnishings, and courses for Gracie.

"But we have a murder to solve."

"It's not going to get solved tonight, Clara. We have a long way to go. I don't want to risk Gracie backsliding."

"She has been making progress," she allowed. "What about tomorrow?"

"I have to stick around here. Assuming Teague O'Donnell shows up to build those shelves."

"He will, but why do you have to be there? Although I understand, what with him being so attractive and—"

"That has nothing to do with it. I am not leaving a strange man alone in my house."

Especially not one inclined to ask nosy questions.

Was I being paranoid about Teague? Maybe. But why did he ask so many questions about me? True, they started before the murder. A hopeful sign he didn't think I murdered Bob Coble.

That still left the major concern about preserving my distance from the author of *Abandon All*.

I wanted to stay here in Haines Tavern. If I were outed as the author of *Abandon All*, would I be able to? Probably not.

So, yeah, possibly paranoid, but some paranoia was justified.

Even if Clara was right that he was quite attractive. Those eyes…

I CALLED MY great-aunt again, before she dove deep into her evening writing session.

I was eating dinner—a salad and scrambled eggs—she was gearing up for work.

After filling her in on the day's scant news, I asked the question I'd called to ask. "Kit, how can you tell if someone is—or was—a cop?"

I'd had the thought at the sheriff's department. It might explain a lot. But it also raised the question: Could he possibly have been planted at the Torrid Avenue Dog Park before the murder? What would have interested anybody then?

The stomach-sinking answer was me.

There'd been short speculative articles about the disappearance of *Abandon All*'s author from the literary scene. Would someone hire an investigator for a scoop?

"Check his or her badge."

Kit being a smart ass was too familiar to slow me. "When they're possibly acting in an unofficial capacity and they haven't identified themselves as law enforcement."

"That dog park of yours? Surely, not your friend Clara."

"No. Why would it have to be at the dog park?"

"Because that appears to be your only social outlet at this point. That is certainly what your mother tells me. She is worried you're isolating yourself and going to turn out to be an old maid like your great-aunt."

"I wouldn't mind in the least turning out to be like my great-aunt."

"Flattery will get you nowhere. Besides you've already got all the money you need. You don't need to be in my will." *Abandon All* had been very good to both of us.

I laughed. "But, seriously, how would you tell if someone was a cop? I have a feeling about this Teague guy. He's always asking questions and it's like he doesn't take things at face value. He doesn't take me at face value. Everybody else has. It's not a situation to ask to see his badge. So how could I—we—know?"

"It's not sure-fire, but start with how he watches what's around him. What and who."

"Yeah. That fits, along with his question-asking."

"There's also a way a lot of them stand. Men and women. I suppose it's from carrying all the equipment. It's a wider stance than normal. Seem more rooted in the ground. Don't shift their feet around as much as most people. Start there."

"Hmmm." I'd have to think about that.

"What kind of questions does he ask?"

I told her.

"You're worrying about being unmasked as the author of *Abandon All*. You could be reading more into it than is there. Besides, does it matter if he's a cop?" she asked.

"It might."

"Because you're interested in him? Because he's interested in you?"

"Not the way you mean. What matters is whether he can be trusted or not."

Clara kept drawing him in deeper and deeper, making us a circle instead of a pair … with the dogs as accessories.

"You think if he was a cop you can't trust him? That sounds backward."

"I certainly don't think it's wise to spend a lot of time around somebody who was a cop."

"This is the guy who is now substitute teaching high school history, right? If he was a cop, it would be interesting to know why he left law enforcement. That's a strange career path."

"The safest path for me seems to be to stay away from him. Trouble is, he's going to build shelves for me."

"Oh, he is, is he?"

"Don't get any ideas, Kit. Are you writing a romance?"

"Even if I am, that doesn't mean I'm wrong."

"There's nothing to be right or wrong about. He's just a new guy at the dog park who knows how to build shelves."

"Who might be an ex-cop, which makes you nervous about whether he might try to find out about your past. There is one good thing, Sheila."

"What?"

"You don't have to worry about if he's interested in you for who you are—or were—the way you always were with men in New York. The fact that he showed interest in you from the start proves his interest has nothing to do with your secret."

Unless he'd been hired to investigate me.

"I told you, he's not interested in me at all and I'm not interested in him."

"The man *is* building you shelves."

"I'm paying him."

"Probably not enough to make that worthwhile unless he's interested in other things."

"Good-bye, Kit. I have to take Gracie to class now."

CHAPTER NINETEEN

ADOPTING GRACIE WAS more work and in some ways more stressful than buying the house. After all, the house was an investment of money. Finding the right dog was an investment of the heart. I could sell the house and move. The dog was with me for the duration.

When I realized I wanted a dog, big and fluffy immediately came to mind. Perhaps this was from a childhood of golden retrievers. And that's where I started. With so many dogs needing homes, I knew I wanted a rescue. I saw four other breeds and innumerable mixes.

None connected with me the way I would have hoped. Maybe I was expecting too much. Maybe I should stop hoping for violins and get a dog I'd grow to love.

And then I saw a picture of Gracie.

What can I say?

It was her expression. A combination of assurance, mischief, sweetness, and a flicker of heart tugging uncertainty.

That began a process I swear was more rigorous and nerve-wracking than college admission. I gathered materials to prove my worthiness including family photos of interacting with our dogs, guarantees that I could support a dog financially, including medical care, and finally a home visit.

If I had realized what was ahead of me qualifying to adopt a rescue collie, my house-hunting would have been more rigorous.

A house that needed all sorts of work? All the construction projects, all the strangers, all the upset? What had I been thinking?

That clearly was the opinion of the collie rescue volunteer who visited my home.

But I was fortunate. Gracie's foster family took to me when I drove the one-hundred-plus miles to meet her. The foster mother went to bat for me with the coordinator and all I had to do was pledge to take Gracie for a walk or to the dog park every day for the rest of her life. With a few get out of jail free days for emergencies—Gracie's emergencies, not mine.

Before I picked up Gracie from the foster family, I read everything I could get my hands on about adopting a dog, especially a rescue dog. I was going to be the best rescue dog owner ever.

Within twelve hours, Gracie had me in tears.

Yes, she had chewed on a shoe, but it wasn't even my favorite shoe, so, really, who cares. And she hardly peed inside at all, plus it was on the hardwood floor so, again, really, who cares.

What had me in tears was that she seemed entirely uninterested in my existence.

That was rather a trick because I'd followed the instructions from several sources that said to keep the dog in a small area with you at the beginning. She had to work at not paying any attention to me.

Once my self-indulgent tears ended and I thought about it from her point of view, I suspected a lot of it had to do with her experiences before I adopted her.

She'd shown up at a shelter at about seven months old. The people there said she'd been abused.

A family adopted her, perhaps with good intentions, but after only a few months they gave her up to collie rescue. It was greatly to their credit that they found the rescue rather than returning her to a shelter. What was not to their credit was that their reason for giving her up was complaining about the dog hair.

They looked at a collie and were surprised there was dog hair?

You have to wonder about some people's good sense.

Gracie's foster mother suspected the family expected Gracie to be Lassie straight out of the gate.

Gracie was not Lassie. For one thing she's female and all the Lassies were male. For another she had a lot of things to do and if

Timmy's in the well, he better get himself out, because chances were she'd be busy. For a third thing, she had trust issues.

I didn't know any of this at the beginning. Those first days, sliding into weeks, were definitely a period of adjustment for both of us.

Our family golden retrievers when I was growing up loved being hugged. Heck, they loved being used as pillows.

Gracie backed off from attempts to hug her, or squirmed out of them. But she loved having her chest, belly, and butt rubbed. The more vigorously the better.

Who was training whom?

Still, I could see progress.

I was getting better at reading her body language.

She was tolerating more petting.

The first day she came into the office on her own and settled by my feet with a deep, contented sigh, was another teary one. For totally different reasons.

CHAPTER TWENTY

I GOT TO Zepke's early on purpose.

It was in a hundred-year-old brick building a block off the square and across the street from the back of the hardware store, with hardwood floors, a resident giant turtle and parrot—who sometimes hitched rides on the turtle, making for a strange double-decker—and an event room in the back where they held classes.

It tells you a lot that, other than dinner at the Historic Haines Tavern, this was one of the happening spots on Friday nights.

Between the front door and the event room came a thousand temptations to the pet owner. At least I wasn't tempted by the racks of sweaters, coats, rain gear, and costumes. I couldn't imagine Gracie taking them with ... well, good grace.

Leo, the instructor, looked up at our arrival.

"Hi, Gracie!" She sashayed over to him at that enthusiastic greeting. "Sheila, how's it going?"

He meant the training, not my life, so I said, "Pretty good."

I had a question about Gracie I wanted to ask, but that would wait. I'd seen other class members parking as we walked in, so I didn't have long before we'd have an audience.

"You've heard what happened at the dog park, Leo?"

"Yeah. Couldn't believe it. Shocked the hell out of me."

"Horrible," I agreed. "Did you know Bob Coble?"

"Not really."

"I thought he might be a customer here."

"Are you kidding?" he scoffed mildly. "He got it all imported."

Of course, he did. "Including that tweed leash? Excuse me—lead."

His mouth quirked at my self-correction. "Yup. I'd offered to special order for him at one point, but then he found out I was special ordering for Dwight, too, and he said he'd take his business elsewhere. Hurt for a bit, because some folks followed him. But I'm glad to say they're almost all back."

"I'm glad, too."

"Now I wish I hadn't. Special ordered for Dwight, I mean." His face darkened. It made me wonder if Dwight was Leo's prime suspect. "I even joked to him in the bank yesterday getting a wad of cash from the teller that he could pay off his bill right on the spot and I'd write him a receipt. He blew me off. I thought he was having a bad day. But now…"

"Have you seen Dwight since then?

"No. Wouldn't have believed it, but…"

"Have you told the sheriff's department about seeing Dwight with all that cash?"

"No. You think I should?"

"Yes."

"Damn."

That's all there was time for, because a basset named Basil came in with his owner then, quickly followed by more. Including additions to the class, taking advantage of Zepke's offer to alums to return for refreshers for free whenever they liked.

They included Donna with her gray-muzzled golden retriever named Hattie. She came and sat next to me, saying, "We're all here pretending it's because the dog park's closed, but it's really to hear the gossip. Well?"

"Me? I'm the total newcomer. I don't have any gossip."

"You found him, didn't you? Horrible for you and Clara."

"It was. But we don't know anything more than was in the paper."

She patted my leg. "Not true, I'm sure, but you're right to tell an old lady to mind her own business. Just—"

"I'm not. I didn't—"

"—watch your back with Berrie. This business has truly unsettled her foundations. Never the firmest in the first place." She sighed. "They had a lot of history. But that's beside the point. She needs to get a grip. If she gets too much for you, ask her if her dogs are French bulldogs. She'll go so far off the deep end, nobody will give credence to anything else she says."

Ah. Another confirmation that Berrie had been saying nasty things about me.

I decided to plow ahead, especially with the circled chairs rapidly filling. "I've heard her say there was some problem between Bob and Ruby?

"Oh, yes. Among other things, Bob wrote a letter to the editor in which he said the post office must have decided people were getting out of there too fast, so they asked the DMV how to keep customers around longer, presumably in the hope that we would be overcome by a lust for stamps or overpriced shipping boxes. Whatever the postal service's motivation, the DMV came through by recommending putting Ruby Zweydorf in charge."

"He wrote that in the newspaper? Named her? And signed it?"

"He did. And she *had* worked for the DMV before moving to the post office. He didn't stop there, either. She aroused his ire some way or another and he began filing complaints with the post office. Caused her no end of headaches. It let up for a while, but I understand it's renewed lately."

As much as I wanted to pursue this, I also wanted to open a couple other doors.

"Was there also something with Amy and maybe some other folks?"

She looked around. "We'll talk again later."

Class began then.

AFTER CLASS, I had to wait my turn to consult Leo with my question about Gracie.

"Why is Gracie slow in responding to the sit command?"

"She's processing. When a dog learns a new command, it needs to process."

I didn't think so. But rather than argue, I gave Gracie the sit command. She looked around. Backed up half a step. Wiggled her bottom. Finally began to fold her back legs. Then slowly, slowly lowered her bottom to the floor, wiggling a bit there, too, like a chicken settling onto its eggs.

The trainer nodded sagaciously. "See?"

"Uh-huh. But ... Wait. Watch this. Okay, Gracie." She hopped up. I took out a sliver of treat she zeroed in on immediately. "Sit."

Whomp. Her butt could have set off a sonic boom. That's how fast it hit the floor.

Leo nodded sagaciously again. "She's food motivated. Makes training much easier." He moved off to the next dog owner.

"Big help," I muttered. How did I get her from food motivated to me motivated?

I heard chuckling behind us. Gracie turned before I did, her tail going a mile a minute.

Teague and Murphy, Clara and LuLu, stood there.

"What are you guys doing here?"

"With the dog park closed, I wanted to give Murphy some socializing."

The free-for-all at my house earlier hadn't been enough? Then I remembered Donna's comment about wanting to pick up gossip. Interesting. Teague O'Donnell was in the gossip biz?

That also reminded me I had more questions for Donna, but when I looked around, she and Hattie were gone.

However, I did spot a four-pawed black and white figure in a red coat disappear around a corner. Most important, I'd spotted its bat-like ears.

A Boston.

Berrie might not be the only Boston terrier owner in the county, but the chances were still good ... I needed to get close enough to be sure she didn't have Marcus with her.

Clara said, "I'm hoping to pick up clues. LuLu's along for the ride."

I said to Teague, "Let that be a lesson in honesty to you. What kind of clues, Clara?"

"Whatever we find. Haven't you talked to people? You've been here an hour."

"It was a class," I protested.

"Where are you going?"

"I want to have a word with Berrie."

"On purpose?"

Teague only partially masked his chuckle.

"I thought it would be nice to express some sentiment that we were both human beings caught up yesterday in a distressing situation."

"Wouldn't have been as distressing if she hadn't tried to throw you under the bus."

Good point.

CHAPTER TWENTY-ONE

IT WASN'T MARCUS.

That was the good news.

I was less sure about good quotient of Clara and LuLu joining us, with Teague and Murphy being barely visible on the other side of this rack of dog toys, definitely in hearing range.

I hurried past Berrie's hostile squint to say, "Berrie, I want to offer my condolences. Amid all the hubbub, your very deep loss has not been adequately acknowledged. This is such a personal tragedy for you. And I want to say how sorry I am for your loss."

You couldn't say it exactly mollified her, but she did speak to me. "I'm glad someone recognizes that, finally. I don't understand why they haven't arrested that horrible man."

"They need evidence," I pointed out. "That means a careful and thorough investigation. There could be a lot of things going on that we don't know about."

"That not *all* of us know about," Berrie said with significance.

I had no idea what she might be referring to. A glance at Clara informed me she didn't know, either. Berrie was zero-for-two. Her hinting stats sucked.

"From what I hear, some might know a lot more than they're saying," she persisted, staring at me.

I blinked at her.

She huffed out a breath. "You were in that enclosure. Your dog found him, like she knew where he was all along. And that deputy clearly suspects you."

Instead of defending myself, my first thought was *Ah, that exasperated huff was impatience that I hadn't recognized her hints*, making her spell out her suspicions. Bad enough the woman accused me of murder. She'd also wanted me to do most of the work of interpreting her hints.

"Sheila? You're saying Sheila—? Why Berrie Vittlow, shame on you." Clara puffed up in anger.

"Well, that deputy—"

"That deputy jumped to a totally wrong conclusion based on not the smallest hint of knowledge of dogs. That's who you're setting up as your new guru? That's who you want to align yourself with? Why, Bob Coble would roll over in his grave—if he were buried yet—and wherever he is, he's surely disappointed in you at this moment. That deputy." She shook her head. "I do believe he is, in fact, a cat person."

"*Cat person?*" I murmured from the side of my mouth. Opening it any further might let loose suppressed laughter.

A muffled sound also came from the other side of the dog treats rack. Teague. That reminded me I'd forgotten to compare how he stood to Kit's description.

Berrie, on the other hand, blanched and recoiled, presumably at the possibility of listening to a cat person.

Clara took advantage to change the subject. "Berrie, you knew Bob so well. Besides Dwight, who had disagreements with him? What about his life away from the dog park?"

"I don't know why you'd think I'd know."

Berrie's quelling tone had no more impact on Clara than the hinting had. "Because you talked to him all the time. Went over to his house—"

"Perfectly respectable, I assure you. We discussed ways to share our experience and wisdom with those not yet educated in creating a partnership with one's animals."

Uh-huh. I'd seen it before, where a death produced almost immediate memory deterioration, resulting in the rewriting of history—especially the history of relationships.

I had no idea if Bob and Berrie's relationship had been anything other than platonic, but it sure as heck hadn't been as colleagues. Bob

Coble wouldn't have permitted that. He was the expert. Always. At least in his eyes. Berrie could be his acolyte, his follower, his adherent.

His colleague or equal? No way.

Thinking about Berrie's shouted words at Ruby and Amy this afternoon, along with the bit Donna had filled in, I asked, "But Bob did have conflicts with people who weren't, uh, following rules?"

"You mean those horrible neighbors of his?"

"Yes," Clara said immediately.

"He tried and tried and tried to get them to see reason. They've been horrible to him. Can you believe it? They called animal control on Trevalyn."

"Was he loose?"

"No. In Bob's own backyard and they still called."

"That's awful." Oops. Clara's protective instincts when it came to dogs might lead her astray.

"What did Bob do?" I asked.

"What could he do?" Berrie responded plaintively. "He showed animal control how well trained Trevalyn is. They couldn't help but be impressed. But their hands were tied. They had to give him a warning. Bob was horrified Trevalyn's record and reputation was besmirched. He did what he had to do, filing that lawsuit."

"What la—?"

I talked over Clara. "Yes. Tell us more about that."

"He was suing them." Berrie shrugged.

Yeah, that was helpful.

"Store's closing in five minutes, folks," Leo called out.

"Oh! And I promised Marcus his favorite treats when we come back."

We had no hope of keeping Berrie's attention after that.

CHAPTER TWENTY-TWO

GRACIE HAD ENERGY to spare on our last-call walk.

She'd had only a few minutes' run at the dog park yesterday and none today. The ring-around-the-rooms and hour-long class at the pet store barely took the edge of her stamina.

So, when she saw a figure walking toward us with a dog, she started to bounce with oh-boy-let's-play excitement.

I had a different reaction.

It probably didn't help that I'd spent the past hour making notes of possible murder suspects and motives, the kind of activity that made you jumpy when you spotted a figure walking toward you on a dark street. Even in Haines Tavern, Kentucky.

"Sheila?" A voice softly called. "Is that you and Gracie?"

I breathed again. It was Amy Kackley and her English setter mix, Sadie.

"Hi, Amy. Don't usually see you out this late."

"I was waiting for you."

That did not induce a warm fuzzy feeling. More like a prickly cautious feeling. "Oh?"

The dogs met with wagging tails and sniff greetings.

"I knew you were asking questions at bunco, but everybody was talking all about the murder last night, so I didn't think much of it. Now, Donna tells me you were asking about Ruby and me tonight." Prickly might be contagious.

But I ignored the caution. "I wondered about what happened at the post office today, with Berrie."

"What happened was Berrie being her unbalanced self. Her and Bob Coble. The two of them deserved each other. Too bad—Well..." She caught herself before saying something I probably would have wanted to hear. "For heaven's sake, attacking Ruby Zweydorf of all people. A nicer, kinder woman you'll never find. And attack her where it could hurt her the worst—her job. You saw Ike in there with her?"

"The man reading the newspaper in the corner?"

"That's Ike. Ike Zweydorf. He was hurt in a car accident about ten years back. He can't talk anymore. Has some other brain damage. Not real bad. Just bad enough that he can't be on his own. Sure can't work. Hates the adult day care that's available. But he's okay sitting in that corner, reading the paper front to back a couple times, knowing Ruby's there, never bothering a soul.

"But Bob—high and mighty Bob Coble complained to the post office about it. Another time he filed an official complaint that she opened two minutes late when Ike was having a real bad day. If Ruby lost this job ... I wanted to stra—"

She cut that off. Though this I could fill in for myself.

Gracie stopped trying to induce older and wiser Sadie to play and looked up.

"It's a saying, Amy. No worries."

She shook her head. At herself, I thought.

"People called me a Dwight out at the dog park. But I've had dogs all my life and I have my own ways. It wasn't so much following Dwight as being an anti-Bob. Wanting nothing to do with him and how he used everything as a weapon."

"Like lawsuits?" It was about as open as a question could be. I hoped Amy would answer it with everything she knew. No such luck.

"Yes."

"What kind of lawsuits?"

"I don't think I should be talking about this."

"Berrie did talk about Bob suing you and Ruby." Amy held her silence. "Lawsuits are public record."

"And you're entitled to check public records at the courthouse. Anything else, it's gossip."

"Can't be gossip if you tell me directly."

Silence.

"There's nothing you can tell me?" I tried.

"What I will tell you is that Bob Coble threatened a lot more law-suits than he ever filed."

Yes, I did notice she changed my *can* to *will*.

A trip to the courthouse appeared to be in my future. But not until it reopened Monday morning. I'd have to add that to my notes.

Along with the note under the big question mark: Where is Dwight?

CHAPTER TWENTY-THREE

THE FIRST THING out of the phone when I answered it right after Saturday breakfast was, "How's Gracie?"

That question could have come from my mother, father, brothers, sisters-in-law, nephews, and niece, though nobody else might know that's what she was asking in her adorable baby talk. It might even have come from Aunt Kit, though not in baby talk. Also not at this hour.

Besides, I couldn't identify this voice.

Though … Had I heard it before? Not too long ago. Not my real estate agent. Not the closing company. Who—? Oh.

"Christy?"

"Yes. Didn't I say? Sorry. It's Christy Yaslowski of Ohio River Valley Regional Collie Rescue." Having rapidly dispensed with the petty details, she returned to the vital topic. "How's Gracie?"

"She's doing fine."

"I was concerned this business might have upset her. When they're first settling in, keeping to a regular schedule is helpful. Routine builds their confidence. Oh, perhaps a few changes to keep them from becoming too rigid or fearful, but within the context of a secure schedule."

This business.

Meaning a murder.

"She hasn't shown any ill effects. But how did you know about, uh, about this nasty business?"

"I saw it in the paper and when it said the name of the dog park, I checked with some connections. That's when I heard Gracie and you were on the scene."

Impressive. "You must have an amazing memory with all the people you meet through collie rescue to remember where I live." She was the rescue coordinator Gracie's foster mother persuaded to let me have Gracie.

"Anyone who adopts one of our dogs is worth remembering."

Put in my place, I quickly said, "Of course. But Gracie is fine. I'm looking at her right now and she's stretched out in a patch of sunlight with her eyes closed, but listening to every word." Christy's chuckle relaxed me. Perhaps too much. "Initially, she was rather keyed up after finding the body and then with all the law enforcem—"

"*She* found the body? Oh, dear. Oh, dear. *That* wasn't in the paper."

I should have kept my mouth shut. Could I try to claim brownie points for keeping Gracie out of the media spotlight? Even though nobody had tried to focus it on her?

Abruptly, I felt like the worst dog mommy on the planet for failing to consider the emotional impact on Gracie. Though her behavior had set me up for failing to recognize potential trauma, what with eating, sleeping, playing, barking, and treat-begging as usual.

"We had class last night. Everything was normal. Honestly, she's been fine," I said defensively. Though did I *really* know that? Maybe I didn't know her well yet. Maybe I was missing signs of trauma or—.

"No, no. I'm not doubting that she's doing well. Especially since Bob Coble wasn't someone she cared about."

"He wasn't. She was entirely indifferent to him and—Wait. How do you know she didn't care about Coble? Did she meet him before I adopted her or—"

"Not that I know of. No, I'm quite sure she didn't. Not the way he talked about her. That's how I knew."

Talked about her? Bob Coble talked to Christy Yaslowski of the Ohio River Valley Regional Collie Rescue about Gracie? He'd never mentioned the group that I'd heard. He'd certainly never told me he chatted about my dog with the rescue coordinator. How—?

"Did he volunteer for collie rescue?"

"Not that I know of. Certainly not for us. But he called us about your adoption of Gracie."

"*What?*" Turning multisyllabic, that word skidded up the scale "When? Why? What did he say?"

"He was quite circumspect, but he indicated he didn't think you were a good owner for Gracie."

"Why that—" I bit off my opinion of the man. As the thought of what I'd like to do to him if I could get my hands on him flitted through my head, it was followed as quickly by the recognition that he'd had a lot worse meted out to him. Considering the man was dead a tongue-lashing ranked as irrelevant.

"He expressed concern about how you were training her and—"

"He is—was—totally and completely biased. Anybody who didn't do exactly what he said was practically an abuser in his book. He had no balance, no reason. It never occurred to him that anybody could be right except him and his own dog is no paragon—" I clamped my mouth shut. I was not going to criticize a dog to get back at a person, no matter how annoying.

Especially a dead person, I reminded myself as my reason trotted to catch up to my emotional response.

It might need to shift to a canter, since I found myself dropped to my knees on the kitchen floor with the arm not holding the phone wrapped around Gracie's neck in a possessive hold that had her giving me the crazy-human-side-eye.

"Oh, we don't take people's word for it. Especially not since I'd vetted you myself. But we can't ignore such calls, either. We enlisted someone to check on you."

Someone to check on you...

"Teague O'Donnell," I said immediately. "New to the dog park, has a lab mix named Murphy."

It had to be him. It fit perfectly. His sudden arrival at the dog park. The questions. The way he kept hanging around with Clara and me. Okay, the dogs might have started that, but he'd probably sprayed his dog with some secret collie-nip that Gracie hadn't been able to resist.

"No."

"A little over six-foot," I pursued. "Light green eyes. Dark hair, a touch of gray."

"No."

I mentally scrambled for other candidates. "Leo, the trainer from Zepke's pet store? Berrie Vittlow, who raises Boston terriers? Dwight Yagos?" He might have told them I wasn't training Gracie right—for the opposite reasons Bob Coble did. Belatedly I realized suggesting a string of people I thought might have been spying on me could come across as a tiny bit paranoid. "You can talk to my family—okay they're biased. But other people will tell you Gracie's doing well. My neighbors. The lady who runs the post office. The woman I hang around with at the dog park, Clara Woodrow—"

"That's the one."

My uptake was so slow, it was like the gears in my head went round and round but nothing turned. I expressed my reaction with a vacant, "Huh?"

"Clara Woodrow. I should have remembered her name. We needed someone on hand. Someone with a good perspective, some experience. And no ax to grind, unlike Bob Coble. Don't think we don't know his type. But we have to pursue any such report, especially while the adoption's still in the six-month probation period."

Probation.

I didn't think my heart could drop any lower, but it did.

"Clara's mother-in-law was my cousin's son-in-law's aunt's best friend." She laughed. "I know it sounds crazy, but we keep a database with connections at dog parks in the region for just such occasions."

That's why Clara made friends with us? To spy on me.

"Probation?" I got out through dry lips.

"Uh-huh. Still five months to go. But sounds like things are going well. I talked with Leo, that trainer you mentioned. He said you have some new-owner jitters, but you're working hard and have good instincts. And Clara's report couldn't have been better.

"They both said Gracie was doing well, despite that awful business. Despite finding a body, as you said. Gosh. Clara didn't mention that.

That's horrible. So, tell me how training's going."

I stumbled something out. The classes. The walks. The milestones of snuggling at my feet. The trips to the dog park that didn't end in finding a dead body.

And tried not to think or talk about probation and Clara and how this phone call might have been very different.

I'd been worrying about Teague's questions, I'd totally missed Clara's observations.

On the other hand, she'd given a good report. And she'd done it for Gracie's welfare.

On the other, other hand, Bob Coble would have said that's what he'd been doing, too, the rat fink.

THE COUNTY NAME of North Bend was a compromise between strong characters in the early history of the area. No, their names weren't North and Bend.

That name comes from—you guessed it—a north bend taken by the Ohio River, surging up to give Ohio an angled corner and Kentucky its northernmost knob, before dividing Kentucky and Indiana in a plunge southwest.

All this surging and plunging by the Ohio River carved out North Bend County, caught between proximity to Cincinnati to the northeast and state solidarity with Louisville to the southwest, while belonging to neither.

My real estate agent had touted a number of neighborhoods—sought-after Blue Grass Estates with all its streets named after famous jockeys, a community in a neighboring county with nice homes packed nearly as closely together as its traffic, another near a park with views of the Cincinnati skyline.

I'd spent fifteen years living in a brownstone in Manhattan. If I'd wanted more of that kind, I'd have stayed there.

I wanted less.

A particular kind of less.

She'd been reluctant to show me this house in Haines Tavern in the "sleepy" part of the county.

"Don't you want to be closer to good shopping? The mall, the town, the services, easier access to Cincy? If you're on the east side of the county you can have all that."

"But this is the county seat," I said.

"Yes." Her acknowledgement made that distinction dubious.

Haines Tavern was the county's original settlement, with its face firmly toward the river as its main thoroughfare. After a couple decades, an upstart community appeared inland to serve the pike from Cincinnati to Louisville.

As if that newfangled road would ever replace the Ohio River as the prime mode of transportation, thought the leaders of Haines Tavern … as so many leaders of so many places have thought about so many new ways of doing things.

The county seat designation was about the last triumph Haines Tavern had over that "upstart," now the biggest town in any of the counties snuggled up to the southern bank of the Ohio River and collectively called Northern Kentucky.

"Stringer has much more to offer," the real estate agent said of that biggest town.

"This house speaks to me." To her continuing doubt, I said, "Besides, it's close to the dog park."

"But you don't have a dog."

"Oh, but I will."

But Bob Coble had tried to take her away from me.

If he weren't dead…

Long after the call ended, I sat on the floor, hugging Gracie.

She didn't even try to squirm away. Much.

CHAPTER TWENTY-FOUR

THE KNOCK CAME at the back door. Gracie barked as if convinced I wouldn't have heard the sound.

I saw Teague looking in as I kept working to make Gracie sit and stay before I opened the door.

After seven attempts, I feared he would freeze out there before I succeeded. I know, I know, dog trainers would shoot me. But they weren't outside my door in sub-freezing weather.

I opened the door, holding Gracie's collar.

"Thought I'd spare your floors by coming to the back door." Teague gave me a searching look. I dropped my head, letting my hair swing forward. "Left Murphy home for the same reason. Also to spare your ears from their wild play."

I turned away as I released her. "I might appreciate that. But you lost Gracie's vote."

She had already sniffed all around Teague and was standing with her nose pressed to the seam of the storm door and door frame as if trying to find a hint of Murphy, hoping this was all a silly trick of the humans and we had him stashed just outside the door.

"Hey, Gracie," Teague tried in a cajoling tone.

She daggered him with a dirty look and walked away. I laughed despite myself and Teague gave a wry half grin.

"Are you okay?" he asked.

"Fine. Want some coffee?"

He hefted a tote bag. "Brought my thermos."

"Okay, ready to get to work?"

"Yep. Going to double-check those measurements before I go buy the lumber and other supplies. Then, if you clear out your stuff to give me room to work, I should be getting started before noon."

"Already cleared out." I led him up the stairs and around the corner to the small office to show my handiwork. I'd put away the files and the boxes were gone. Yes, the bookshelves were triple stacked, but that's what he was here to remedy.

Good to his word, he was off to the hardware store or lumber store or wherever he was going to get the materials in a little over half an hour and back by eleven.

He set up a saw in the half of the garage not occupied by my car and produced annoying but productive noise at irregular intervals.

I brought Gracie with me to the basement, where I found chilly but not as noisy work to do—laundry and putting away tools received as Christmas presents from my father and brothers. I needed them.

Then I called my mom.

✧ ✧ ✧ ✧

I TOLD HER all about the call from the collie rescue coordinator. Well, not all. I left out the part about the guy who'd reported us—Gracie and me—being dead and us finding his body.

At the end, she said, "Nobody's taking Gracie away from you."

Which made me feel better.

Then she said, "You should move closer to us."

Oddly, that also made me feel better. Of course, it's wonderful to be wanted, but even more, it was so predictable, so dependable, so Mom, and I'd needed that.

"I just moved here."

"Do you think I don't know what's going on there?"

"What do you mean? What's going on here?"

"A murder. At the dog park you take Gracie to. A *murder*, Sheila. That wouldn't happen here."

"Of course it would or could. Plus there's that murder they always whispered about in the church steeple—"

"That's history. Ancient history. Or legend. It's not real. It's not now. But you found that man's body two days ago. You and Gracie and your friend."

"How do you know *that*?"

"Not from you, clearly." That sounded tart enough to remind me that my usually laidback mother was related to Kit. "Do you think I don't keep track of what's going on in Haines Tavern now that you've moved there?"

"But it's only been in local news."

"Exactly. I subscribe to Haines Tavern news and your neighborhood forum. Like I do for your brothers."

"Mom, that's a little extreme."

"Obviously not, since you have had a murder there. I don't think it's safe for you to be there."

"But Mom—" I cut it off because I'd been about to argue that I'd already dealt with a murder a few months ago during my transatlantic cruise. Before blurting that out, I recognized that would not have been a persuasive argument with my mother.

She didn't seem to notice my false start. "I'm just glad your father doesn't know."

So was I. If Dad's My-Baby-Girl mode kicked in, I'd have to bar the door to keep him from trying to move me out of my house and back under their roof, where he could stand guard.

"Mom, the sheriff's department is investigating. They're all over this case. They'll have it solved in no time." I kept my reservations about Deputy Eckles to myself.

"You should talk to Kit."

I didn't mention I already had because it undercut my story that I was relying completely on the sheriff's department. "At this hour? You're the one who said that if she ever saw a sunrise it was from staying up all night."

"That's true. She got in the habit of writing at night when she had to work a full-time *normal* job and she never broke it. Night's her creative time."

"Exactly. And morning's her sleeping time. If I called her now it might be the end of a beautiful relationship, and it wouldn't gain me any usable information."

"Later then, but call her. All those mysteries she's written, maybe she has connections who know about the case. But if Kit says it's dangerous for you there, that's the end of it. You're coming home."

Mom didn't know Kit was living—and loving—this investigation vicariously through me. No way would she want me to leave.

I could use the I'm-a-grown-woman argument another time.

"SHEILA?" TEAGUE'S VOICE carried down the stairs into the basement. "You have a visitor."

Upstairs in the kitchen I discovered my visitor was not a curious neighbor, as I'd guessed, and had brought Gracie's favorite toy— LuLu. Gracie was making full use of that toy by chasing her around the circular pattern. Whose bright idea had it been to buy a house with a circular pattern?

"Clara, what's up?" I thought I sounded normal and Clara didn't seem to notice anything different in my tone.

"I thought we three could talk about the case while Teague is working."

"Trouble is," Teague called from the stairs, "I'm working."

"We're also not in charge of this investigation," I pointed out.

Clara, removing her coat, waved one hand which caused the sleeve to flap in a dismissive gesture. "Not in charge, but we agreed we were going to look into it." Did I hear a sound coming from the stairs? "Besides, we can always help Teague if he gets behind from helping us."

"No, you can't." Teague's shout was buffered by coming down the stairs, but emphatic.

"No, we can't," I said on the heels of his words. "I'm paying him. If I wanted to do the work myself I wouldn't hire someone else."

"Nonsense. Watching will help you learn what to do if you want to do it yourself next time. Besides, you heard Berrie last night and you know she's feeding stuff about you to the sheriff's department."

"I never had a problem—a real problem—with Bob before he

died." *Now* I had a problem with him.

"Except at the post office, when he got all outraged about Gracie being inside," Clara said.

"That wasn't a real problem," I protested.

"Maybe not like Ruby had with Bob, but it did get heated."

"Heated does not mean I'd murder the guy. But what—"

"Oh, I know that. I didn't mean to imply—"

"—is this about a problem between Ruby and Bob?" I felt wounded and distanced from her, but I wouldn't pass up the chance to use her as a resource.

"—that you would. Bob got upset with her one day because she asked those questions they have to ask every time you mail something about if it's anything dangerous and Bob said it was stupid of her and a waste of time for her to ask those questions. She told him she had to because of the regulations. He—"

Teague came around the corner, clearly drawn by the conversation.

"—studied all the regulations and reported her anytime she broke one. Nothing important or dangerous, just small, petty rules. One time, he even reported her when she was trying to do him a favor."

This wasn't much different from what Donna and Amy had said, but did add details. And possibly depth to a motive for Ruby?

"Everybody told him that was not only petty, but self-destructive. He didn't care. He said if she was going to live by the rules, she was going to die by the rules." She sucked in a small gasp. "Not that he meant... Besides, he was the one who died. Oh! I'm not saying Ruby—"

"I know. Though, it's interesting they had that history even before—"

Cutting off my own words did no good. Teague raised one eyebrow. "Even before your run-in with Bob Coble at the post office about Gracie?"

"How did you know about that?" Clara asked.

"Small town. Even a newcomer like me hears things. And you can count on the sheriff's department hearing more."

"Well, if that's the only reason for looking at me—and there can't be any other reason—that's a lot weaker than a lot of other people, especially Dwight."

Clara's eyes widened. "You haven't heard?"

"Heard what?"

"He's missing."

CHAPTER TWENTY-FIVE

"Deputies went to Dwight's house—finally got around to it last night—and he wasn't there. His SUV is gone, too. None of his neighbors know where he could be. They haven't seen him for days."

"How did you hear this?"

"My grandmother used to live next door and one of the neighbors called me to get her phone number in Belize—"

"Belize?" I quickly waved off my own interruption. "Never mind. Go ahead."

"Anyway, the neighbor told me the sheriff's department questioned everybody up and down the street."

"Canvassed."

At that mutter, I turned to Teague. A cop would certainly know the distinction between someone being *questioned* and law enforcement going through a neighborhood checking for anyone who knew anything. But I cared less about that at this moment than another aspect. "Did you know he was missing, too?"

"Does it matter?" he asked.

"Depends on how much earlier I could have known."

"What are you going to do with the information now?"

That was a challenge.

"Clara and I are going to go talk to her grandmother's former neighbors and find out what they told the sheriff's department as well as anything they might not have told them."

She picked up her purse. "And then we're going to see Ned's

cousin's ex-wife. She's having a few neighbors over to meet us."

"She lives near Dwight, too?"

"No. She lives catty-corner from Bob's house."

HAVING TEAGUE COME along was not my idea. But since these were Clara's connections, I felt I couldn't interfere when she asked if he wanted to join us. I could—and did—give him a cool look when he accepted. He tried, without success, to look innocent.

"All your family members live around here, Clara? You and Ned seem connected to everybody one way or another," Teague said from the backseat.

Clara abruptly looked into her side mirror. Was she embarrassed? Thinking about the family connection that led to her spying on Gracie and me?

"They're pretty much all around here. And yes, we have a lot."

"What does Ned think about you looking into a murder?"

"He's happy I've found something I'm so interested in."

"I'd like to meet Ned."

"Great. We can all have dinner. That'll be fun. But he's busy with work right now, so maybe in a few weeks. I'll let you know."

"He doesn't know what you're up to, does he?" Teague asked with entirely unwarranted skepticism.

"Oh, look. Here we are."

Dwight's neighborhood was on the cusp between suburban and rural, with small houses set well back in large lots. Here and there an old farmhouse proclaimed itself an original settler.

A sheriff's deputy's cruiser sat in the long driveway of the house Clara indicated as Dwight's.

The neighbor who'd called Clara, a woman in her early sixties, lived two doors down. She started by describing everything she'd seen the deputies do the night before and the questions they'd asked her.

"Those deputies have it all wrong. They couldn't make up their minds whether Dwight went off on a lark or if he killed that man at the dog park, then skedaddled. Makes no sense. No sense at all. Why, he had a houseguest just before this for several days. What kind of person goes from having somebody staying in their house to murdering somebody else?"

I doubted that reasoning would impress Deputy Eckles. It didn't do much for me, either. Perhaps she sensed that. Because she shifted her approach.

"Well, I don't see him murdering anyone any way anytime. But *if* he did, he wouldn't leave like this. He'd stand up to what he'd done. And never did hear of him taking a trip like that. Leaving his grandmother and—"

"Skeeter," she, Clara, and I said together.

"Is anybody taking care of—?"

"Now, don't you worry, Clara. Neighbor on the other side of Dwight's got Skeeter. Heard him howling and took him in."

She'd precisely recapped the arguments against believing Dwight had taken a spur-of-the-moment trip. First, no one had ever heard of him going anywhere. Second, he wouldn't go without Skeeter. And third, he wouldn't leave his grandmother without her caregivers knowing where he was.

Of course, that assumed that they *didn't* know…

I made a mental note to check that.

CHAPTER TWENTY-SIX

CLARA'S HUSBAND'S COUSIN'S ex was Molly Brackenhurst. She and her new husband had lived near Bob for a decade.

She'd gathered eight other neighbors. Most were in their forties or fifties. Except a couple who sat at the back and were younger than me.

The woman seemed familiar, yet I couldn't place her. Maybe she had that kind of face. She had chin-length brown streaked hair and was dressed half a level less casually than the rest—her top appeared to be silk, rather than polyester. Her apparent significant other had a shaved head, fashionably darkened chin, and wore a cashmere V-neck over a t-shirt.

They did nothing to draw attention to themselves, including speaking.

Molly did enough of that for everybody.

She and her neighbors had plenty of complaints about Bob. From the mundane of his yelling at her kids if their ball or other toy inadvertently crossed into his property, to his lodging complaints with the homeowners association about their garage being disorganized.

"Really? He complained about that?" I asked.

"He said that when our garage door was open, he had a view of it from his front window and that it was disreputable and unpleasant and ruined the *prospect*."

That sounded like Bob Coble.

"What happened?"

"We agreed to try to keep our garage door closed." She chuckled. "But we knew we wouldn't be perfect, so my husband also gave him a controller to close the door if it ever bothered him."

"You didn't worry about him closing it at an inauspicious time?"

"You mean like on one of our kids? We weren't too worried about that. It has one of those seeing eyes so it won't close when there's something in the way. Like a kid when his brother tries to squash him under the door. Besides, as weird and picky and cantankerous as Bob could be, he was never cruel to kids and certainly not to dogs. We had an old lab up until four months ago." Tears glazed her eyes. "Bart had a much harder time getting around those last few years, but he loved being with the kids, he would try no matter what. A year-and-a-half ago Bob showed up at our door with one of those wheeled contraptions that helps a dog whose rear legs have weakened. He wouldn't let us pay him back. He didn't say much. Except about the right way to use the wheels, of course. But I would see him in his window watching Bart and the kids.

"Nobody can tell me Bob Coble was all bad. A pain in the ass, yes, but not all bad. Whoever killed him, they could have left Trevalyn to die, too."

"Oh, my gosh." Clara half stood. "How long was he alone?"

Molly waved her back reassuringly. "He's fine. From what the deputy said, he was alone all night and most of the day."

"Where is Trevalyn now, Molly?" Clara asked.

"Animal Control."

"No," Clara and I chorused.

"If no one else takes him, I will," Clara said.

"And break LuLu's heart? She's the princess and she does not want competition." Molly patted Clara's arm. "We're already seeing if we can adopt him. I wouldn't be surprised if other people on the street might be interested, too. No matter what people thought about Bob, they love Trevalyn." Her eyes flickered. "Most of them."

The woman in the back shifted in her seat.

That movement shifted the lighting on her face. I recognized her.

She was the woman in the cloche hat from the post office.

I had a hunch.

✧   ✧   ✧   ✧

"BUT THERE WAS an incident with Trevalyn that led to a lawsuit, wasn't there?" I looked directly at the couple.

The woman flinched. The man spoke. "Wasn't the dog. It was him—Bob. He got all wound up about dandelions in our yard blowing seeds into his. We've got kids, we don't want chemicals, so sue us."

"He did," muttered one of the men. That drew a few chuckles, apparently emboldening him. "And your dandelions do blow seeds all over. I've had to double treatments to get rid of them."

Molly held up a hand. "Let's not get into that again."

"Bob sued you?" I asked the couple. Molly frowned at me, but I ignored it.

The man looked angry. The woman looked … guilty? That seemed weird.

"He could file as many lawsuits as he wanted, that didn't mean he'd win."

"Bob complained about the dandelions. You told him to get lost. He complained to the homeowners association. You reported Trevalyn for something. He piled dog poop near your entry walk. You—"

"How do you know all that?" the bald man demanded.

"She's got the pattern," the man who also didn't appreciate dandelions said. "And then Bob would sue."

The man stood. "C'mon, we're going," he ordered the woman with a head jerk.

They left.

But the floor had opened to complaints about Bob. It seemed Molly and her family got along with him the best. Most of the other neighbors were somewhere between them and Rosie from bunco who'd been glad to leave him behind as a neighbor.

✧   ✧   ✧   ✧

"YOU GOT QUIET there at the end, Sheila," Teague said to me.

"You were quiet the whole time."

"True. So that could be seen as my natural state. But for you, it was a sudden change. What caused that change?"

"I was shocked I hadn't factored the dogs into all of this, Trevalyn and Skeeter."

"You mean Dwight wouldn't waltz off for vacation and leave Skeeter, which he wouldn't," Clara said. "For that matter, neither would Bob. With Trevalyn, I mean."

"Somebody running after, say, committing a murder, wouldn't be thinking clearly. They do things you wouldn't expect. Things they wouldn't do otherwise," Teague said.

Clara was having none of it. "Dwight would not have left Skeeter even if he had killed Bob. Even if he were running for his life, he would not leave Skeeter. I don't think he would have left Trevalyn to suffer that way, either, without food and water and someone to rescue him."

"For what it's worth, based on the short time I knew him, I agree with Clara."

"Is that all you were thinking about?" Teague asked me.

"I said it was."

CHAPTER TWENTY-SEVEN

WE DROPPED TEAGUE at my house to work on the closet shelves.

I'd intended to get out of Clara's SUV there, too. But Donna called as we reached my street. She invited Clara and me to join her at Historic Haines Tavern for tea.

Having missed lunch, I wasn't passing up a meal.

Who am I kidding? I wasn't passing up a chance to hear whatever Donna had to say.

THE WREATH ON the front door of the Historic Haines Tavern offered a lot more hope for spring than the temperature did with the sun dropping fast.

Inside, the main dining area opened to the left, with more up the stairs that shared the center hall with a passage to the rear. To our right was the tap room.

Clara headed through the tap room, I followed. Between the fireplace topped by a large oil painting of a glorious horse and the polished wooden bar backed by a period mirror and array of bottles, she entered a doorway that led to a hall.

An employee greeted her by name, knocked on a door, then gestured us in. The room held four wing chairs, a round pedestal table given over to tea, tiny sandwiches, pastries, and Donna and Amy.

Donna welcomed us warmly. Amy's face remained tight.

With the door closed and each of us occupying one of the comfortable chairs, Donna poured cups of tea and passed them around.

"I thought we might have a meeting of minds in this convivial setting," she said.

As the newcomer, I kept my mouth shut by occupying it with a raspberry pastry.

"This is very convivial," Clara said, "but what do our minds need to meet over?"

"All this poking around you're doing," Amy snapped. "It's the sheriff's department's job."

"We're trying to fill in answers that aren't part of their investigation. They don't know everything that we do."

"Then tell them." Still snappish, Amy had backed off a few notches.

"They haven't listened. They didn't even check on Dwight until last night. Now they can't find him anywhere."

Donna and Amy stared at her, then looked at each other.

"Dwight's missing," she emphasized. "And Skeeter was left alone in the house."

Amy sucked in a breath.

"Have you heard from Dwight, Amy?"

"No. Left a message but—"

"I know. His mailbox was full."

Clara recapped what we'd learned, but only about the dogs. Ending, "See, there are lots of things the sheriff's department doesn't know about, doesn't care about."

"To them, the Torrid Avenue Dog Park is a crime scene. To us it's so much more," I said.

Amy stiffened again. Maybe I should have stuck to the pastry.

Donna gave me a sideways look. "Why do you always say the whole name? Most of us just call it the dog park."

"I love the name. So many possibilities. Scandalous possibilities."

Amy gave a tight smile. "Pretty boring, actually. I looked up the history when we put together a display at the library on the town being on the national register of historic places. Torrid is the southern boundary of the original town as the founders laid it out. Temperate is the northern boundary, Sunrise the eastern boundary, and Sunset the western boundary. Pretty simple, really."

"Rather poetic," Clara said.

"Totally disappointing. I'm holding out for a scandalous explanation," I said. "They made up a respectable reason to tell the historical people."

"Well, there were a number of bars and taverns on Torrid Avenue," Amy said. "I found letters by one of the founders who said Hezekiah Haines used all his influence to have Haines Tavern be the only one right at the center of town. By the late 1800s, when they decided they needed to build a new and bigger jail, there were comments in the newspaper that building it out there would be convenient, because most of the jail's occupants came from those taverns."

Donna sniffed. "Apparently forgetting about the trip to the courthouse for their legal rights in between."

Amy met my gaze for an instant at the mention of the courthouse, with its connections to Bob's lawsuits.

"Different times," she said. "They forgot all about that, too, when they used the Hanging Tree. There are pictures of it in the archives. Including a couple with someone hanging there."

Clara gasped. "That's awful."

"People took things into their own hands," Amy said with significance. "Sometimes you might be able to say it was people thinking they were doing right, but far too often you can see in the records that people knew it was wrong. Jumping to hang someone as the person they labeled the *obvious* culprit to short-circuit the legal system."

I bit my tongue to keep from defensively saying that wasn't what we were doing.

"There were two famous instances. They hanged a young black boy, not even fifteen years old, for robbing a store when some of those who participated admitted later they suspected the ringleader of the hanging was really the one who committed the crime. That ringleader took off right after. Word was, he went to St. Louis and died there in a bar fight. His widow—well, his wife when he deserted her and their children—did so much better with the farm than he'd ever done and she employed most of that young boy's family members, making one a manager at a time that was unheard of."

"Small compensation," Donna muttered.

"All that the woman could give them," Amy said.

Donna nodded acceptance.

As interesting as that bit of history was, I couldn't see how it possibly helped us, but wasn't about to say that. Amy was visibly relaxing as she talked.

"The other case was brother against brother over a woman. Both wanted to marry her. Her father said no to both. The father's murdered, and a man's seen fleeing the scene who resembled the brothers. One declares the other did it. Swears up and down he's heartbroken over it, but can't bear to hide the murderer of his true love's father. And he turns his brother over to a mob of the murdered man's relatives, who hang the accused brother."

"Good heavens, I've lived here all my life and never heard these stories," Clara said.

"This is the history that doesn't get told."

"Kids would probably like school better if they were," I said.

"I hope that surviving brother got killed in a bar fight or worse," Donna said.

"No. He married the girl. They still have descendants in the county." A sly glint sparked her eyes. "By the name of Coble."

CHAPTER TWENTY-EIGHT

SHE GOT ALL the reaction she could have wanted. Though it turned out Bob was descended from a cousin of the two brothers.

Amid the dwindling exclamations, Amy looked at her watch, folded her napkin on the table, and stood. "I have to get back to the library. I'm working until closing."

The door closed behind her after our good-byes.

"You did well." Donna looked from Clara to me and stuck there. "You gave her a chance to decompress. She won't go to the sheriff's department now and tell them you're interfering with their investigation."

"Was she going to?" Clara demanded.

"Oh, yes. I hadn't persuaded her otherwise and she was braced for you to argue against her. By not arguing, she had time to consider the point on its own merits, not only in opposition. Not opposition to you, but to what's happened. She feels Bob did great injustices, particularly to Ruby. She also has little sympathy for Berrie."

"The woman scorned," I murmured. I added for clarity. "Someone at bunco referred to Berrie as the woman scorned in connection with Bob."

"Her business—" Clara said.

At that same time, Donna said, "Oh, that. Ancient history."

Both stopped and looked at each other. Then both exhaled a *huh* that acknowledged the legitimacy of the other's comment.

"You go first," Donna invited.

"Okay, but only because I think that will save the best for last,"

Clara said. "Berrie's trying to start that dog training business. She said she'd learned so much from Bob that she was sure she could help other people as he helped her. Bob wasn't as enthusiastic. In fact, he was downright nasty."

Donna nodded at Clara's assessment.

"He said she could barely tell a dog from a rat, which was mean, taking a side swipe like that at her beloved Boston terriers. He also said her people skills were even worse than her dog skills, which were nonexistent. And then, there was…"

Clara and Donna exchanged a significant look. "Don't leave me in suspense," I begged.

"That happened at the end of summer," Clara picked up. "Then, in the fall, Berrie had that website designed to promote her business. Cost her a fair amount. Bob heard about it, he made a lot of harsh comments. First, to her in person at the dog park and then on the website. After a few days, she disabled the comment feature and deleted everything he'd written. They had a screaming match at the park a couple weeks before Christmas. He said he would sue her if she didn't remove every mention of him. She'd had sections where she talked about what she'd learned from Bob and how much she admired him. It was all very complimentary, but he didn't want to have any association with it.

"That was his right, but he was so snotty to her. He didn't need to be. She's been his most loyal follower and he acted as if she'd dirtied his name by saying nice things about him. He could have handled the whole thing quietly, without embarrassing her to the point of tears."

"Tears of hurt? Or embarrassment? Or rage?"

Clara looked toward Donna, then shifted in her chair. "All three, I suppose. She told me she put quite a bit of money into that website. Then she had to spend more to remove the references to Bob as well as his comments. And she can't afford it. She hoped dog training would rescue her finances, instead of costing her even more."

"She's spending a lot more money than she has on those Bostons." Donna clicked her tongue. "She takes in any rescue they can't find a spot for. Which does her credit. But she also needs to be practical and reasonable. She's got to stop taking in more dogs. Without training credentials I don't see how she expects to earn much—or anything— from that website or training in person."

"She thought she could earn off the website?" I asked.

"Yes, she was offering training tips remotely. Troubleshooting dog behavior with advice for a price from people emailing her. Don't look at me that way, Sheila. It's not my idea. I'm reporting what Berrie planned." Clara finished her tea.

"Has she had customers?"

"Not off the website. And I can't imagine what happened is going to help her efforts to find local customers. Augustine, the woman with the German shepherd, was freaked out."

Weren't we all? "How bad is her financial situation?"

Clara looked toward Donna, clearly inviting her to answer.

She flipped her hand, palm up, indicating uncertainty. "All I can say is I've heard she keeps her house cold and lights on in only one room to save on utilities."

The dog park offered inexpensive entertainment, but the dogs required food and healthcare, not to mention treats and toys. Her Bostons clearly had all of those.

Could Berrie have felt threatened enough by the obstacles Bob presented to her business hopes to have wanted to remove him?

"But she's been loyal to him, one of his true followers."

"They made up over Christmas, at least to some extent. What you've seen with Berrie's attitude toward Bob has actually been quite subdued. Really. You should have heard her before their falling out."

No, I shouldn't have. Not if she was more fulsome than she had been the past month.

"Do you—each of you—think she would have, could have, killed Bob? Because that's what we're talking about."

After a pause, Donna said, "What does Berrie care about the most? The Bostons. If anyone, even Bob, threatened their well-being in her mind oh, yes, I could see her attacking the perceived threat. Would she plan out a murder? No, but she could act in the moment, realize what she'd done and try to cover it up, try to protect herself."

"I absolutely agree with Donna. Especially… Well, that's Donna's part of the story."

I turned to the older woman in expectation.

"It's not all that thrilling, but Bob and Berrie were, indeed, once an item. A couple."

"But I thought…"

"Exactly. Most people probably do think Bob's gay—was gay. I'm not so sure. Some people simply aren't that interested, you know, no matter what their orientation is."

"But didn't he and Berrie date when they were younger? I heard they had but never the details." I stared at Clara. She hadn't bothered to tell me that?

"They did. The end of high school, some in college. I suppose he could have done it because it was what was expected. Their dating certainly was what you would expect, especially in Haines Tavern all those years ago. Groups going to movies, dances, trips into Cincinnati, swimming in the summer, skating in the winter." Donna smiled with nostalgia and sadness. "But I suppose you mean the details of their breakup. I'm telling you this because I know you're not wanting to gossip and you won't spread it. Under other circumstances I wouldn't tell you at all. But… Bob is dead." She squared her already squared shoulders. "If Berrie had nothing to do with it this can't hurt her and if she did… Well.

"I don't believe Bob did break up with her. Not outright. He just stopped asking her out. It drove her wild, trying to figure out what happened. Left her thinking it was something lacking in her. That she hadn't been attentive enough, hadn't played the girl-boy game well enough. Maybe, with her insecurities, she would have thought that no matter what. Some women do. But with him drifting away into indifference, she kept trying harder and harder. It wasn't pretty. She mooned after him. She derived encouragement from the fact that he didn't have relationships. Certainly there were no apparent liaisons—not with men or women. She saw that as an opening for her, instead of the futility of trying to work an infertile field. In that way, it was very sad. All these years of her trying so hard. But she also brought it on herself. She *refused* to see. And she was relentless. She'd manufacture excuses to be around him, to spend time with him.

"When his liking for dogs became an obsession, she followed right along. But, miracle of miracles, her obsession focused on Boston terriers and that superseded her obsession with Bob."

"How did he take that?"

"A perceptive question, Sheila. He was relieved. Absolutely. However, at some level, I also believe, it put his nose out of joint."

"What makes you think that?"

"He got more and more testy with her the more independent she became. Though independent might not be the best way to describe it. She was so far the opposite of independent…" She tapped her hands on the table. "I suppose I should start at the start. Her parents died one right after the other while she and Bob were dating. Bob became the center of her universe. And that didn't change even after he stopped asking her out. He was the center of her universe, while she was merely a small, side planet in his. But when she adjusted to orbiting around the Bostons, he discovered he missed being someone's sun. He'd never have admitted that, but I believe it was true."

"I didn't know either of them until after all that," Clara said. "But I can see it. I wondered why she was loyal to him when he often wasn't nice to her. He wasn't like that to his other followers. He at least recognized their loyalty. But she was more loyal than anyone else and he showed no appreciation at all. Like being so harsh about her website."

"Complex relationship with all that history," I said.

And it made Berrie a viable suspect.

Her alibi for the night of the murder was the Bostons.

But who was I to talk? Mine was Gracie.

Donna eyed me. "You're thinking it could lead to murder? But it can also lead to the kind of love and devotion that would never consider murder, even if it some might consider it justified."

CHAPTER TWENTY-NINE

CLARA CAME **IN** with me. She also came upstairs to see what progress Teague had made.

After admiring the stacks of shoe boxes outside my closet awaiting a home, she stuck her head in the closet. "Wow, Teague. You could do this for a living if you didn't want to teach."

"I want to teach. Went back to school so I could teach after I retired."

Retired from what? He'd had the slightest hesitation before the word *retired.* Was there something there? Kicked out? Forced to retire? It couldn't have been too long of a first career because he wasn't senior citizen age. But he could have put in twenty or thirty years in the military, then—

"That's right. You started to tell us about that before. What was your first career?" Clara asked.

Well, sure, if you were going to ask outright for the information instead of trying to figure it out … What was the fun of that?

"I was a cop. Retired as detective."

OH, C'MON. **WAS** that fair? Sometimes the universe has a perverted sense of humor.

A cop, okay. I'd braced for that.

But a *detective*?

Really, you're going to make a retired cop—a detective, no less— be the owner of the dog that my dog adored?

How was I going to explain to Gracie that we couldn't go to the dog park anymore because her buddy's human's previous profession made him Haines Tavern's Most Likely to Unmask her human's hidden past? The dog's smart, but that's getting a little deep, even for her.

"Why'd you leave law enforcement?" Clara asked.

"Pursuing other interests."

He was hiding something. Maybe it takes one to know one, but I was sure. "Such as?" I asked with tea party politeness.

"Dog training." And he said it with a straight face.

Clara groaned. "Like the dog park needs another one."

"True, so what did you learn at tea? Solve the whole case?"

"I wish. We should all sit down and strategize—"

He interrupted Clara. "Sorry, I'm tutoring. Gotta get going. Mind if I leave my equipment in the closet?"

"No problem."

I needed to consider the implications of his detective-ness.

I also wanted to have a private word with Clara.

Turned out, that was mutual.

✧   ✧   ✧   ✧

SHE SAT AT my dining room table, rubbing Gracie's ears.

"Sheila, I know Christy from collie rescue talked to you. Told you I … Well, I was watching you." She brought her head up, met my eyes, then dropped hers. "Spying."

"That's why you introduced yourself."

"Yes. I probably would have anyway because I'm a friendly person, but, yes. I went to the dog park on purpose for three days in a row to meet you before you brought Gracie the first time. After that it was … easy."

I said nothing.

After a long silence, she went on, "I know you probably can't forgive me for how we met and I don't blame you. I did it only to make sure a dog was okay. Gracie." She bent over and put her face in the generous fur at the back of Gracie's neck. "I'd do it a hundred times over now that I know how wonderful she is, to make sure she was okay. But I am sorry if it means we can't be friends."

Before I could say anything, she spoke again.

"But I don't think you should let this stop us from trying to find out what happened with the murder. It's too important. And I think we're making progress. Really, making progress."

I didn't answer directly.

"Clara, if you and I talk about Bob's murder and potential suspects, that's one thing. But I don't think you—we—should talk about it with other people. Especially strangers."

"Strangers? I haven't talked to any *strangers*."

"Teague."

"He's not a stranger."

"You've only talked to him a few times. First met him, what? Three or four days ago?"

"So? You're probably at about the same number of times talking to him." She said that as if it proved her point that we did know him, instead of mine that we didn't. Then her expression turned expectant. "Unless you've talked to him more times I don't know about?"

"No. No, I haven't." Ignoring that moment in the grocery store and his hand so close to touching my hair. "Neither one of us has talked to him hardly at all when it comes right down to it. So, I wish you wouldn't be so open with Teague. We don't know him. He showed up at the dog park a few days ago and we don't know anything about him except what he's said."

Like me.

I better get her past these points before she applied them to what I'd told her about my background.

Secrets, truths, and lies. With my own still intact, how could I not forgive her for hers?

"But he's a cop—law enforcement."

"How do you know that?"

"He said he is."

"Exactly. *He* said. That's no proof. Anybody can say anything."

Again, just like me.

I had to stop thinking that.

"We need proof. Evidence. Look at the timing," I said. "Teague shows up at the dog park and—boom—Bob is dead."

"No, no, you're wrong about that, Sheila. He showed up after we found Bob dead."

"I didn't mean the day we found Bob. I meant overall. Teague arrives at the dog park the first time, what? Three days before Bob was killed? Did anything else change in Bob's life before he was killed? That would be a very interesting thing to know. But even if you're only talking about the day Bob was killed, Teague could have killed him the night before, then come back after he saw us arrive and knew someone was likely to find Bob. So, he could see what was happening, but wouldn't be the one who found the body."

Clara turned to me with admiration in her face. "That's really good."

Did I believe it? Let's say it was a possibility. Slim, but a possibility.

If it kept him at more of a distance because Clara didn't trust him, that was all to the good.

"So, you'll be careful around Teague now? Not include him in our conversations?"

"I think we should check him out. I'll get right on that."

Why did I feel I had not come out ahead in this conversation?

CHAPTER THIRTY

"**WHEN ARE YOU** coming home to see us?" My mother employed her favorite conversation starter the next morning, Sunday.

"When are you and the rest of them coming down to see me?"

"There are three families of us up here, getting everyone organized…"

"First, even with three households up there, it would be fair to gather at my place every fourth time. Second, there's no need to get everyone organized. Whoever can come down, comes down. Of course, if somebody doesn't come down for a long, long time, they're going to be in big trouble, and you can tell Robbie that."

"Now, Sheila—" Though she didn't call me, Sheila. I'm using that to not make your head explode the way mine sometimes wanted to do, because she used the name I'd gone by in childhood, which was also different from my *Abandon All* name. "—don't be hard on your brother. They have young children and that's a very demanding time—"

I snorted. "What's been his excuse the rest of his life?"

"I know you're testy only because of that horrible situation down there."

"I'm not testy. And I told you, the sheriff's department is handling it." Possibly handling badly, but handling it.

"I know. That's what Kit said when we talked yesterday. She says I'm worrying unnecessarily."

"You are."

"But she's not a mother."

Always her trump card. But bringing up the sheriff's department had given me another idea. "There's also an ex-cop—a detective, actually—who's one of the regulars at the dog park. So, he'll certainly keep an eye on the investigation. In fact, he's doing carpentry work for me. Building shelves."

"Oh?" That's all it took to know Mom's focus had shifted.

For once, I didn't try to shift her away. I let her ask, "Ex-cop? Where is he from? Is he married?"

"He's from the Chicago area. Doesn't seem to be married. He's retired—"

"Oh. Retired."

In my mother's mind, Teague had gone from a dashing possibility to a gray bearded old fogey. If I wanted to maintain his status in her mind as a viable protector, I needed to do repair work.

"I guess he put in his twenty years then retired."

I should have asked him yesterday why he'd retired. Had substitute teaching been such a dream for him? Was that what was behind his pause before *retired*? Or was there another story there?

"Twenty years?" Mom was doing the math.

"He's substitute teaching. High school history."

"Isn't that what you decided to tell people…?"

"High school English."

She sighed. "I do wish you didn't have to lie."

"I know. But it's part of the package that has given me a very good life for the past fifteen years and set me up for the rest of it."

"That's what Kit keeps saying."

"And she's right. Do you want to see my investment account statements?"

She responded to my teasing with a chuckle. "No. I know you and Kit would not kid about something like that. I also know that while you talk about it giving you a good life, you have also given Kit a good life. She is now taken care of in ways we never could have dreamed of. The whole family is grateful for that, even though most of them don't know the ins and outs."

She, Dad, and my brothers knew I hadn't written *Abandon All* and its followers. No one else. Not even my sisters-in-law, who'd come along after *Abandon All*'s publication. Though they did know I had now dropped that life for a new one.

Sometimes things got very complicated.

CLARA WAS CALLING me.

The instant I answered the phone, and with no hello, she said, "Word is the dog park opens at one. If I don't get LuLu out there she's going to explode and take my house with her. My sanity, too."

I hesitated for a beat. "Gracie, too. How soon can you get there?"

"On the dot at one."

THE FIRST TIME I took Gracie to the park, she was somewhere between wary and aloof. Until she and LuLu did the butt-sniffing dance and came out of it besties forever. If one of the dogs wasn't there, the one at the park moped so much Clara and I had been forced—really, forced—to arrange playdates.

We usually went earlier in the day when there were fewer people there.

That sounds more antisocial than we are. Well, Clara's not antisocial at all. I'm the one hanging back.

The more time that passed since my disappearance from the public stage as the author of *Abandon All*, the lower the chances of someone making that connection. In the meantime, no sense taking chances.

The upshot was I didn't know most of the people congregated at the Torrid Avenue Dog Park.

And Clara—drat the woman—was late.

It was jammed. Because of the murder or because of pent-up dog energy that could power the county?

Probably both.

It didn't help that only one enclosure was open. Both large-dog areas and the small-dog one Berrie favored were all still taped off.

Marcus rumbled some bass register Rs when Gracie and I entered the enclosure, but that was on his way to greet us. Once he reached us, he quieted. That was a shock. Had he been saying all along that he wanted us to join him in their enclosure?

He and Gracie congenially schnuffled each other before she flitted away to find a more active companion. I'd track her more carefully than usual in this crowd.

Berrie was only a few feet away. I could ignore her, but…

"Hi, Berrie."

"Sheila." She hadn't looked up since we'd entered the enclosure, so that meant she'd spotted me earlier.

Gracie found Murphy, not far from where Teague talked with Donna.

"Berrie, why didn't you use your regular enclosure?"

"It's not open."

"Not today. The day we found Bob."

Despite still facing her boots, her voice strengthened nearly to usual Berrie throttle. "I was working a large dog. And it wasn't as muddy."

"Ah. Makes sense." I cast around for something else to say. "These have been difficult days."

"That cretin deputy thinks I'm a suspect—*me*. You have no idea what that's like."

Oh, I had some idea, thanks to her.

"Did you see it?" No pause allowed—or forced—me to ask Berrie what. "That article was simply riddled with errors. Describing Bob as *a* top trainer in the tri-county area? Unbelievable. He was *the* top trainer. And as his closest ally and student, now I am. They didn't even include that or my name."

"It was Bob's obituary, Berrie."

"That's an excuse. Like the reporter saying they wouldn't run a retraction because it quoted some idiot at the humane society. I called his editor and demanded a retraction."

I pressed my lips together to keep from saying that no doubt Bob would be the first to wish for a retraction of his obituary.

I saw a flash of Gracie, turned to follow it and received the gift of

LuLu face to face.

She achieved this position by planting her front paws on my chest. Her wet, muddy paws. Leaving imprints that resembled—I recognized as I looked down at myself after LuLu dropped to the ground then trotted off to join Gracie and Murphy—paw-print pasties on my light gray jacket.

"You shouldn't let LuLu jump on you that way," Berrie said with censure strong in her voice. "She'll never treat you as leader when you let her do that. Turn your back when she jumps, so you don't give her positive feedback."

"She *had* her back to her," Clara said. "Oh, Sheila, I'm so sorry. Can I—?" Her hand fluttered toward my chest. "Or maybe that'll make it worse?"

I strongly suspected that, yes, a woman being seen rubbing my breasts, even through a jacket, at the dog park would make the situation worse. "It's okay, Clara."

"I'll wash it or take it to the cleaners or replace it."

I started to respond, but Berrie was not to be denied. "You have to anticipate. To know your dog so well you're always two steps ahead."

"LuLu is not my dog. And I needed eyes in the back of my head to anticipate that."

A group started to gather around us.

"I train dogs all the time that aren't mine. Anticipation has been a key element in my success. And it's especially important with a dog who presents a danger."

"Danger?" Clara repeated in blended astonishment, insult, and disdain.

Several spectators gaped at the idea of LuLu, an acknowledged clown, being a danger.

That didn't stop Berrie. "What you need to do is be more of a leader. If you'd followed Bob's methods, you'd have strong commands now. You, too, Clara," she tossed off. "Fortunately, I learned so much from Bob, I can work with you—"

"If it's such a great method, why hasn't it worked with Marcus?" came a mutter from the back of the group.

Berrie spun toward the voice. "Was that you, Nathan? You and Dwight always were thick as thieves. You probably conspired with him to murder Bob. You—"

"That's enough."

Donna's familiar voice cut through rising rumbles, but it was Teague O'Donnell who shouldered in. I hadn't realized the group had tightened so much around Berrie, Clara, and me. Teague's physical presence widened it.

Donna joined him, and he enforced more space by stepping back. I did the same thing, opening the circle. I noticed several of the Sane Middles positioning themselves beside some of the most ardent Bobs and Dwights.

"There's been too much said today already," Donna said. "It's a hard day. It's very crowded, which is hard on dogs and people. So, if you can't stay here without keeping your hard thoughts to yourself, I suggest you go home and come back another day. But leave your hard thoughts home! They're as bad as ticks."

That drew some chuckles.

A few grumbles rose.

"C'mon, now, all of us packed in here have churned this ground enough. Let's let it be. Just let it be." Her listeners could take that as a reference to the soil ... or more.

She shooed at a few people, but turned back and said in a low voice, to Clara, Teague, and me, "You three get down the other end, make sure there's no congregating of one faction or the other."

We did as we were told, watching Donna slowly separate, remix, then herd selected packets of dogs and people. Gracie would approve.

CHAPTER THIRTY-ONE

"SO, YOU CHECKED up on me."

Clara and I looked at each other, at him, then back at each other.

"What makes you think that?" I asked after too long a pause.

"Got a call from a buddy of mine."

Clara started to say something. I cut across her with a drawled, "And?"

His turn to look from me to Clara and back. "And he said a nice lady was asking about me. He got all excited, too. Had to tell him to quit his Cupid fantasies because the caller's married. Happily married." Without moving anything else, he slowly, slowly slid his gaze toward Clara. "Aren't you, Clara?"

She was toast. "Me? Why would you think it was me? I'm sure you know any number of women who might call to see if you were telling them the truth."

"Ah, but he said a nice lady, a true lady, and they're much rarer. I thought of you right away."

That flustered her—deny she'd called or protest the compliment? Which to do first?

"Your friend couldn't possibly know she was a true lady. And—and he couldn't possibly know who it was who called." Triumph came into her face. "Not unless she told him her name."

"She didn't need to." His voice dropped low and soft. A snake charmer's croon. "I know it was you, Clara. I know."

"How? How could you possibly know?"

His voice didn't change, but the lines around his eyes dug deep with suppressed laughter. "Caller ID, Clara. Your name and number came up on his caller ID."

She said the word most of us at the dog park euphemized to poop. First time I'd heard her use it. "What an idiot I am."

"Not at all." Teague grinned, but didn't let out the laughter lurking. "Proves you'd have a lot of sneaky to learn to become Mata Hari."

She huffed. "I'm not sorry I did it."

He slung an arm around her shoulders. "I'm not sorry you did it, either. It was good thinking. Showed initiative. As it turns out, it was a good thing for me, too."

"Really? How?"

"My buddy you talked to—Harris—got curious and looked up Haines Tavern and found the news of the murder. Somebody he was in the academy with is in the sheriff's department here. Harris gave him a call and vouched for me."

"Hadn't you already told them you were a cop?" Clara asked.

"I did. They didn't seem overly impressed with what I told them before. There's something about a murder that makes everyone suspicious. And a suspect."

"But now they should be impressed, with the good old boy network vouching for you," Clara said.

"Hey, not so old."

"But still the boy network," I said.

He shrugged slightly.

Clara frowned at him. "What did you tell them before?"

"Just my observations. Maybe a few impressions."

Talk about raised suspicions, mine circled up around the top of the flagpole. "What kind of observations and impressions?"

"In addition to the confrontation between Bob and Dwight, they asked about you two. I said both of you seem to be nice people. With wonderful dogs."

"And?"

"And you were intelligent and observant, aware of interactions between people at the dog park, as well as the dogs—"

"I'm sure that impressed them."

"—and that you, Sheila, seemed aware of police procedures in cases of unnatural death."

Uh-oh.

The other time I'd encountered unnatural death—a much nicer way to say it than murder—I'd explained my knowledge of police procedures and interest in murder investigations by my credentials as an author. A supposed author.

This time I couldn't use that excuse.

So why would an ex-English teacher be interested in police procedure and murder?

From up at the gate, Donna called out and waved to us. Maybe six dogs other than ours remained. They and their people seemed calm.

We waved back to Donna, acknowledging we'd been relieved from duty. Donna and Hattie left.

"I dated a cop," I said impulsively. Teague's sharpened look immediately told me I might have ventured from the frying pan into the fire. I veered away and added, "And I've always wanted to write murder mysteries."

"You have?" Clara said. "Me too. I love reading them. And I've always thought writing them would be so fascinating. The problem is, I don't know how to write. I mean, of course I can write. But not books. It amazes me someone can start a book and get all the way to the end and have it make sense."

I bit my tongue to keep from saying that sometimes it didn't. Sometimes the author had to work and rework and re-rework drafts, the writethroughs, then edits to get the book to work from start to finish.

"Seriously?" Teague asked.

"Oh yes," Clara said. "I've even read books about writing, but they didn't help. It still seems like magic."

"Sorry, Clara, I meant about Sheila dating a cop. A detective?"

That could explain my knowing things I actually knew from helping Aunt Kit and attending research events with her. But I did quick mental calculations of likely career advancement and ages, especially since I might be better off putting this supposed relationship several years in the past. That would make it easier to be vague.

"No. But his father was. Family dinners were fascinating. Whatever he recommended Sam read, I read, too."

"That's so amazing," Clara said.

Teague did not look nearly as impressed. "With all that delving into his profession, it's a shame it didn't work out between you and your boyfriend. What happened?"

"You'd have to ask him." I infused that with confusion and philosophical sorrow, leaving a neon Do Not Trespass sign over my supposed wound. Not to mention that I had covered why I had no explanation for the breakup.

Brilliant, if I do say so myself.

"Teague," Clara said, "now that we know you're a cop—ex-cop—and the deputies here know it, you can tell them more and they'll have to listen."

"I told them everything I saw. They seem to have developed their own theories."

He said that very precisely.

"We know all about their theories. When we tell them to look for Dwight, they don't. They hardly even blink when he comes up missing," Clara said darkly. "As much as I hate to be really looking at him, it makes sense he would have strangled Bob with his leash. That tweed leash he was so proud of—"

"Wait." I held out a stop sign hand to Clara, but kept my eyes on Teague. I'd seen something there. "The leash. You don't think that's what killed Bob?"

"I don't know anything about it. Outside my scope. Not to mention none of my business. None of *our* business."

I squelched the urge to say *Speak for yourself.*

What if I was right? What if he didn't think the leash killed Bob? That sent my head for a spin.

"It is our business. And you can tell them Sheila didn't—" Clara started.

"They're only interested in what people—including me—know. Not theories."

"But you know Sheila."

"No, I don't." He looked right at me when he said that.

"You know she couldn't have done it."

Before he responded, I turned. "C'mon, Clara, let's go."

"But … But…"

"It's okay, Clara. He's right. He doesn't know me."

We started away.

I stopped.

Clara looked at me questioningly.

I turned back to Teague. "When you separated Bob and Dwight that day they argued, you focused more on Dwight. Was that solely because of size?"

Teague narrowed his eyes, apparently thinking back. When he didn't say anything for a while, Clara said, "Bob started it, jabbing at Dwight, but Sheila's right. You kept your eyes on Dwight."

"Dwight escalated." Then he repeated, "Dwight escalated. And…"

"And?" I prodded after another pause.

"Bob was set up for pushing and shoving. Dwight was ready to go. Hands fisted. His stance. He was ready to fight."

Clara gave a little crow.

His mouth quirked. "All right, all right. That's an observation. I'll talk to the deputies again."

"As long as you're talking to them, ask if Bob's body could have been seen from the small-dog enclosure Berrie usually used."

"I will."

He joined us as we walked out.

CHAPTER THIRTY-TWO

CLARA PEELED OFF to her vehicle. A few parking spaces down, I prepared to do the same.

"Sheila?" Teague called.

"Yes?" I stopped until he came close enough to speak quietly.

"Just so you know, I don't think Clara was the only one who checked up on me."

I did pretty well, saying with a tinge of amusement, "Did you ever consider you might be paranoid."

He gave a half-amused *huh*. "Comes with the territory. Doesn't mean I'm not right. About you checking up. And about thinking you wouldn't leave an obvious trail."

"As flattered as I am by your confidence in me, I'll say—or *any* trail since I'm not doing anything."

"Wouldn't hurt if you did. Women should be careful. Especially about men they allow in."

It was as if he'd heard Kit and me talking. And he agreed with me.

After a couple extra beats, he tacked on an addition that changed his meaning, "Allow in to their houses to do work. You shouldn't count on Gracie as your only protection."

I gladly followed that path, rather than the previous one, which might have been a figment of my imagination, anyway. "I don't. She'd sell me out for the first offer of a treat."

"I doubt that, but bad guys wouldn't hesitate to get her out of the way."

Yikes. Now I had to worry about protecting my dog if she ever tried to protect me.

"We're not in the big city anymore," he continued, "but bad stuff happens here, too, as we both know."

When I thought about that conversation later, it was that last line that bugged me. *We're not in the big city anymore. … We're.* I'd told him I'd worked in upstate New York, *not* the city. So why include me?

Unless he meant him and Murphy.

There was a reassuring thought. Or a straw I'd grasped.

Not so reassuring.

On the other hand, he couldn't do what Clara had. There was no former employer he could call to check up on me. He'd have to call every "upstate" high school. That would keep him busy.

He couldn't be that nosy.

Besides, he'd be calling all those places asking about the wrong name.

✧　✧　✧　✧

CLARA LOOKED AT me. It reminded me of the look Gracie gives me right after she wakes up from a nap which has followed a full day of fun and activity. It's the look that says she's ready for more.

"That was good, right? Not telling Teague I was following you home to find out what we should do next? So what *is* next?"

Slowly, I said, "I think we should do something charitable right now."

Her face fell. "Not sleuthing?"

I didn't answer directly. "Do you know who is probably the most confused and sad and worried and lonely right now?"

"You mean with Dwight missing?" Her frown immediately lifted. "His grandmother. And my grandmother used to live next door to her, so it would be natural for me to visit her."

"Perfect."

CHAPTER THIRTY-THREE

DWIGHT'S GRANDMOTHER SOUNDED determined, but scared when she invited—or ordered—us to come in to her room at Kentucky Manors.

Coming here explained one item—Zig-Zag was the name of the road it was on.

Mrs. Yagos' door opened from the hallway into a neat, sunny room with a bed area on one side and a sitting area on the other. Doors indicated a bathroom and closet. Mrs. Yagos sat in a large chair by one of the two big windows. She had iron gray hair pulled back in a bun.

I saw the strong resemblance to Dwight. But also had the impression of hard edges not so much softened as eroded by time.

"Mrs. Y? It's Clara Woodrow. Trudy's granddaughter? You might not remember me—"

"Of course, I do, child. Got a note from Trudy a few weeks ago with some photos."

She'd gained vigor as she talked.

Clara went to her and took her hand. "That's why we came. This is Sheila Mackey. She knows Dwight, too, from the dog park. We wanted to come say we hope you're not worrying too much because everybody's looking for him. We'll find him safe, don't you worry."

Mrs. Yagos gave a mild snort at that. It could have meant any of a dozen things.

She peered at me with faded blue eyes. I went close and offered my hand.

"Hello, Mrs. Yagos. I'm Sheila."

After a moment, the strain around her eyes eased some. She took my hand in a surprisingly strong shake.

"You here to tell me more nonsense like that deputy tried to that my grandson's on the run from the law?"

"Not at all."

"Well, you better not be. Because Dwight's a good boy. He's probably off somewhere fixing up the final papers and all with some business from last week."

"What kind of papers?"

"Papers so he doesn't need to come running to me all the time. He can just handle things himself."

"Where would he go to fix those up?"

"I don't know. That's why Dwight's taking care of it." I suspect she'd aimed for defiant disinterest. It came out more querulous.

"We went by the house the other day," Clara said chattily. "The neighborhood's not the same without you and Gran, Mrs. Y. Of course, Dwight keeps your house up nice. Can't say the same for the people who moved in to Gran's house."

"Dwight showed me pictures and videos." She clicked her tongue. "It looks strange without Trudy's flamingos. And those curtains on the front porch? Whoever heard of curtains outdoors? Not to mention it looks like you're trying to hide behind them so nobody who's walking past can say hello. What sort of neighbor does that?

"I suppose Dwight's had that dog of his all over my furniture. Skeeter's not a bad dog, but dogs are meant to be outside. I grew up on a farm and dogs worked as hard as anybody else. At the end of the day, they stayed outside or in the barn where they belong. They sure weren't princes the way they are these days. Absolute nonsense.

"But I will say, that's the only thing I know to say against my Dwight. Other than being dog crazy he's a good boy. And there's nobody who can say otherwise. Got a lot of friends that boy has."

"Oh? Who are his close friends?"

"I don't know names." Or didn't remember them, I suspected. "Never took a list or anything like that. He's a grown man. But he'd come home from that dog park and say what this one or that one learned from him about how to keep a dog doing what it's supposed to be doing." Her eyes went unfocused for a moment.

I opened my mouth, but Clara made a small wait gesture with her hand so I shut it.

"Amy. Amy what works at the library. She's somebody he mentioned that I remember. She's spoken to me about Dwight being real smart with dogs. Said so last time I was in the library. Don't get to the library anymore. They bring books to us, which is okay, I suppose, but it's not the same as getting to look up and down the rows. Used to like to get magazines a lot. All those pictures and didn't have to spend a dime. Now I can't hardly see the pictures anyway."

She waved to a framed group photograph on the dresser. "Can't tell light from dark, dark to light anymore. You remember, Clara. Remember how I could see a bird a mile away?"

"You could. And a little girl getting ready to step into the creek in her Sunday best. You called out and I was sure it was the voice of God…"

While they reminisced, I looked closer at the family photo. The Yagos clan has some strong genes, because the resemblances were strong. I was pretty sure I picked out Dwight in the back row until I saw a guy on the right side. Two young women, one with dyed blonde hair, another with deepest black could be identical twins.

Can't tell light from dark, dark to light anymore.

If Mrs. Yagos meant telling those two apart, I didn't blame her.

"…but we're talking your friend's attention right away," Mrs. Yagos said.

"I'm enjoying hearing about when you lived in that house and before Clara's grandmother … left."

Mrs. Yagos gave a cackle. "Wish I'd left for the same reason Trudy did. Got a note from her a few weeks ago with such photos. Was showing them to Dwight…"

Clara frowned at me. "Gran went to Belize with her boyfriend."

Oops. I'd jumped to a conclusion, thinking Clara's grandmother no longer occupied that house because she'd died. Shame on me.

Our hostess snorted. "Eighty-year-old boyfriend. Like they're teenagers. That fella doesn't know how a grown man should act."

Trying to repair my standing with the woman, I said, "But Dwight does."

"Yes, he does. He's a good boy, Dwight is. Not like the rest of them."

"You have other grandchildren?" It seemed likely from that photo, and it might be a good topic to get her talking more openly about Dwight.

"If you can call them that. Never around. Never remember my birthday. Never remember Mother's Day. Never remember nothing except what they want from me, which right now is to die. But they'll find out soon enough that won't get them anything, either. Not them and not my son and not my daughter. Only one who'll get anything is Dwight. Because he's the only one who's given anything. All this balderdash about him going off somewhere and nobody knowing where is nonsense—Dwight wouldn't do that. He'd tell me if he was going somewhere."

"They've been looking for him," I said gently.

"Then they're not looking in the right places. And that's fine with me, because Dwight must not want them to find him."

"It's important he talks to the authorities," I started cautiously. "The sheriff's department would like to talk to Dwight about a man named Bob Coble, a man Dwight didn't get along with."

"I know who Bob Coble is. Heard enough about him. And don't go pussyfooting around with me, young lady. I know he was killed. All that mush mouth about wanting to talk to Dwight is just being afraid of saying they think he killed that Bob Coble. Not so. Absolutely not so. Anybody who thinks so is an idiot. And I'll tell them to their face that exact thing, anybody here—"

The sting to those words made me guess somebody had said something. And likely regretted it after Mrs. Yagos finished with them.

"—or anyplace else who wants to say such a thing. Dwight is a *good* boy. That Bob Coble gave him plenty of trouble over plenty of years. All sorts of nasty things said, but Dwight took it like a saint. Why, I'd tell him give the guy a fist and that would end it. Bob Coble would have run off like one of those dogs with his tail tucked between his legs. But Dwight wouldn't hear of it. Even when he was most aggravated, at the end of all, he'd say, *But to give the man his credit, he does like dogs.* When a boy like Dwight says something like that about another man, he's not going to turn around and murder the fella."

"If Dwight were to hide someplace do you have any idea where it might be? Did he have a special place?"

"No special place, but my Dwight and his cousin explored every inch of that creek runs behind my place as boys. Goes from one end of the county to the other."

A perfunctory knock, then Mrs. Yagos' door swung open to a brisk woman followed by two uniformed aides.

The woman in the lead stopped dramatically, pretending to be surprised to see us. "Who are you?"

I bridled on behalf of Dwight's grandmother's. This brisk woman with Geraldine on her name tag acted as if the older woman weren't even here.

"They're my business and none of yours," she said, proving she didn't need any bridling on her behalf. She could do it quite effectively on her own. "Go away."

"It's time for your treatment."

"Oh, bother. And it's not a treatment, it's a shower. For heaven's sake, call it what it is."

One of the aides giggled. Brisk Geraldine glared. The giggle ended. The other aide simply looked weary.

"C'mon, Mrs. Y," said the giggler with a warm enthusiasm that made me like her. "I've got new smelly stuff for you to try."

"All right," the old woman conceded, but with a brightening interest that made me suspect she looked forward to trying new smelly stuff.

Clara hugged Mrs. Yagos and I shook hands with her before the aides led her into the bathroom.

Geraldine demanded again, "Who are you?"

Before Clara could answer, I said, "It should be clear to you from Mrs. Yagos' reaction that she knew and welcomed us."

"We have to look out for our residents. Not all of them have good judgment."

"Mrs. Yagos does."

"That's so, Clara," came Mrs. Yagos' shout from the other room.

Geraldine—clearly an administrator of some kind—couldn't argue that Mrs. Yagos didn't know us after she called Clara by name. She retrenched. "We've had reporters—and worse—trying to get in to see Mrs. Yagos since this distasteful business at that place they call a park."

"The Torrid Avenue Dog Park." I said it because I thought it would bug her.

She wrinkled her nose like she might have gotten a whiff of poop from the dog park miles and miles away. "We're trying to prevent her being annoyed at this difficult time."

"She didn't take care of the reporters herself?"

"I sure did," came the shout. "I like that one, too. That friend of Clara's."

The aide's giggle followed again. I might have been inclined to join in, except Geraldine's expression killed the desire to giggle.

Geraldine held the outer door open for us in command—brisk command.

Once she closed it with all of us on the hallway side of it, she herded us toward a glass-enclosed office. "Come in here."

"No, thank you." I put a guiding hand under Clara's elbow and encouraged her to keep moving past the doorway. "We'll see you later."

"You're not—"

"When we come back to visit Mrs. Yagos again."

CHAPTER THIRTY-FOUR

BUT OUTSIDE THE building, I slowed Clara.

"Let's go around by the staff entrance. I spotted today's staff schedule on Geraldine's office door and it showed two of the aides getting off in a few minutes. If one of them's the giggler, we might be in luck."

We were.

✧ ✧ ✧ ✧

WE SPOTTED HER as soon as she came out, but it took us a minute to get out of the SUV. She'd almost reached her car when I called out.

"Hi, Carolyn?"

She spun around. "Oh, you startled me. I thought you'd left."

"We're on our way out," I said as we caught up with her. "We hoped to have a word with you. You are so good with Mrs. Yagos and that makes us both feel better, knowing she's well cared for."

"She's a great lady and you two did her a world of good. I don't care what Geraldine says." She giggled again. "Don't tell anyone, but some of us wait until she goes home at night and then we do all the fun things with our people. They love to sing their old songs and dance. Sometimes we go pretty late. Geraldine comes in the next day and she can't figure out why everyone is tired." Another giggle. "It makes it so working days with her is like a punishment compared to the fun nights." She released a little sigh. "At least visitors come during the day, so that breaks it up for our people."

"We were concerned. Clara, here, is a long-time friend of the family, as you could tell. She's known Dwight forever." I fudged that last bit a little.

Clara gave me a look that would have signaled her surprise to someone watching closely. But she managed a nod.

"We heard Dwight hasn't been here for a few days and hasn't even called his grandmother," Clara said, "so we wanted to check on her, see how she was doing. From seeing you all upstairs we knew you would be the one who would tell us the truth."

She looked at us for a long moment. "You two are the ones who found that man at the dog park, aren't you?"

Clara hesitated.

Having a good feeling about Carolyn, I damned the torpedoes and went full-speed ahead. "Yes, we are."

"Some people are saying Dwight might have done that, but I don't believe it."

"Neither of us believe it, either."

Another bit of a stretch. Because if the choice came down to believing Dwight killed Bob and other people thinking I had, I was all for picking Dwight. But if cops could lie to get information, couldn't amateurs, too?

"Mrs. Y is worried. Really worried. He's always here most every day. Rarely skips one. I've never known him to skip two. And now it's been days and days. Mrs. Y is a little confused about time, but she's deeply worried, though she will not admit it.

"A deputy came and tried to talk to her. He upset her, not like you two. He was saying things about Dwight being a suspect in a murder. Geraldine came in and kicked him out, said he had to have a warrant or subpoena or something. He said he'd come back, but he hasn't. Not yet anyway."

Geraldine had redeeming qualities after all.

On the other hand, it was good to know Deputy Eckles was looking at people beyond me.

"When was the last time Dwight came to visit his grandmother?" Clara asked.

"Wednesday."

The day of his confrontation with Bob. The day before we found Bob's body.

"Anything unusual that day?"

Carolyn stared over my shoulder, clearly thinking back.

"Dwight didn't seem like himself. He's usually cheerful with his grandmother. Sometimes you could see him steeling himself to be cheerful, like he hadn't had the best day. But that day, he didn't say hi to any of us, didn't ask us how she'd been. Went right in and they stayed in her room. That was different. He usually makes sure she comes out and socializes. Even if she's not real open to it some days, he can get her to come around. Like I said, they enjoyed—enjoy…"

She came to a stop. I wasn't sure I was the one to nudge her. After all I didn't know the family. Sure, Mrs. Yagos liked me, but that was only on our first acquaintance.

"What was Mrs. Yagos like after he left that day?" Clara asked.

I almost cheered.

"She didn't say anything specific. She was talking about her family, like she often does. She doesn't like her children or the other grand-children. She was saying Dwight was the only one worth anything and most of the rest were worth less than nothing. She talks about that, a lot." Clara nodded agreement. Carolyn continued, "They used to be after her all the time. Calls, letters, once in a long while a visit. But it was all to try to get something from her. They'd start all smiles and loving, because they wanted her to fork over. She wouldn't. And then came the shouting. And those people could *shout*.

"While back, she said she'd had enough. She was too old to deal with them. She told Dwight she wanted him to have power of attorney, to take control. He didn't want to. She insisted. And it finally happened."

"When was that?"

"Week or two ago. She also wanted to sign a new will, giving eve-rything to him. He did hold her off on that. Said she might change her mind. And seems he was right about that. Because when he brought it up Wednesday, she was the one saying not yet, not yet, when she'd been all gung-ho before. But maybe the power of attorney thing has done the trick. From what I know, she hasn't heard a peep out of those others." A mini-giggle. "But that didn't stop her talking trash about them. So, that wasn't anything out of the ordinary."

Watching her carefully, I saw worry squelch another giggle.

"But something *was* out of the ordinary? What?"

"He didn't stay as long as usual and she was real down after he left. Like maybe she was feeling bad for Dwight about whatever was bothering him."

"Any idea what was bothering him?"

Surprisingly, she giggled full out. "Probably that Kentucky lost a basketball game."

CHAPTER THIRTY-FIVE

"WHAT DID YOU think, Clara?"

"I think I should have been visiting Mrs. Yagos all along. I feel so guilty. I'm going to go home and call Gran. Not only to say hello, because it's been too long, but to be sure she's been in touch with Mrs. Yagos."

"All good things, I'm sure. I'm going to call my great-aunt Kit, too." Though I doubted Clara's Gran consulted on murder inquiries. "I meant what did you think of what Carolyn said."

"Oh, about Dwight? It didn't surprise me. It's what I would have expected to hear about him and how he is with his grandmother."

"Yes, it matches what you said about him. That makes me wonder even more if he would have disappeared on his own. Even if he killed Bob, would he have deserted his grandmother?"

"Or Skeeter. And I say, no."

I nodded. "But if he didn't disappear, what happened to him?"

"I don't know. But I do know if we don't leave now, I won't have time to get home, give Ned dinner, and be at yoga."

✧　✧　✧　✧

SUNDAY NIGHT YIN yoga was supposed to be an hour of stretching and relaxation to let us all decompress before the beginning of another busy week, going into Monday morning with a good attitude.

I felt like a fraud, since my Monday morning would be like all my other mornings. That didn't stop me from going. I liked the stretches and time alone with my thoughts.

Though, right now, my thoughts were about murder.

I felt the disturbance of air beside me as Clara placed her mat next to mine, but didn't open my eyes.

"Have you heard?" Clara asked in an urgent whisper.

The whisper was because the other dozen-and-a-half people in the room were stretching or already stretched out on their mats, awaiting the start of class. There was no rule against talking, but it was understood this was a time to sink into mellowness.

"Heard what?" I whispered back.

"Dwight is dead."

I popped up to a sitting position. Heads whipped around toward us. So much for decompressing. Much less zen.

"How? When? What happened? How did you hear this?"

"They found him a little while ago out by the railroad tracks. They're saying a probable suicide. I don't believe it. He would not commit suicide. I'm positive he wouldn't. Especially with Deputy Eckles saying it was all premeditated—killing Bob, then planning to run away, but losing his nerve and killing himself instead."

"Premeditated? Why does he think—? No, wait." I think I knew the answer. The wad of cash Leo had seen Dwight withdraw from the bank the day before we found Bob. "Answer the other questions first. How did he commit suicide? When? Did he leave a note?"

"I don't know any of that. Like I said, they just found him. His neighbor called me. Not the one you met, the one on the other side who has Skeeter. But I can tell you why I don't think he killed himself. Mrs. Y. Skeeter. He wouldn't. I don't care what Deputy Eckles says—"

"Good evening, everyone," came the voice of our instructor. "Welcome to yin yoga."

"Good evening," most of the people chorused back, a few giving our corner of the open room distressed or disapproving or dirty looks.

"—he wouldn't have left Skeeter or his grandmother."

CHAPTER THIRTY-SIX

I WAS A lost yoga cause.

I usually am, but that class was particularly bad.

The instructor often talks about bringing mind and body together on the space of the mat, thinking of nothing beyond it.

My body was there.

My mind was on suicide.

Possible suicide.

And murder.

If they'd just found Dwight, had he committed suicide recently—as in after Bob Coble's murder. Remorse? Horror at what he'd done? In other words, an admission of guilt?

It all fit.

I had to admit, I spent most of the ten minutes of sleeping swan—four minutes or so each side, plus the time to get into the position—projecting pictures where the North Bend County Sheriff's Department determined the evidence proved that scenario.

The case would be wrapped up and I could sink back below anybody's radar. My secret stayed safe.

It was after child's pose—never my favorite, with your face smashed into the mat—as we moved into half saddle, that the reasons to doubt suicide surfaced.

✦　✦　✦　✦

"KIT, HE'S DEAD."

I called her as soon as I got home from yoga. Clara had wanted to come over to thrash out this development, but couldn't. She and Ned had a date each week to watch "their" show together after yoga.

"You told me that."

"Not Bob. I mean yes, he is dead. But I mean his rival, the prime suspect, Dwight. He's dead, too. We knew he was missing. Clara and I went and saw his grandmother and she and an aide where she lives now confirmed he had not been to visit her. Now the sheriff's department has found his body."

"Where? How long ago was he killed? Is there a gap from when he was visiting his grandmother to when he was likely killed? What is—"

"Wait, wait I'm trying to write this down."

"You know all this. You know the questions to ask."

I put down my pen. She was right. "Somehow it makes more sense when you say it."

"When it comes right down to it, you've had more hands-on practical experience investigating a murder than I have."

"Gee, you know exactly what to say to cheer up a girl." And I meant it.

"A fact. Now, let's get back to it. Tell me about this suspect turning up dead."

I did. Also about our trip to Grandmother Yagos. And the phone call from the collie rescue group, ending with "…probably strengthening my motive in Deputy Eckles' mind, I'm afraid."

"That's okay. It means you're well motivated."

"That's the problem. This deputy thinks I *am* well motivated and that's without knowing about Bob Coble red-flagging me or whatever you want to call it with the collie rescue group."

"I meant you are well motivated to work on this case."

"I was working on the case. I didn't need more motivation."

She didn't seem to hear that. "Why is it bothering you so much that this deputy might consider you a suspect? You said you were considered a suspect on the cruise and that didn't bother you much."

"It *did* bother me. But I'm not sure I ever thought the chief security officer *really* considered me a strong suspect. Besides, I was more optimistic the chief security officer would recognize the error of his ways than I am about Eckles."

"You'll have to show this deputy the error of his ways if he doesn't see them himself. What about this former detective?"

"What about him?"

"Can't he talk to the deputy or does he think you're a suspect, too?"

There was a thought. Great. Maybe Teague was working in my house waiting for my homicidal side to show itself so he could nab me.

As if her thoughts had followed the same track, Aunt Kit said, "You better hope Clara stays alive and well, especially if this deputy finds out she was the rescue group's spy."

"*I'm* not telling anybody. But, really, anybody who would think I would kill somebody over that..."

"People have killed for less."

"Thanks for that vote of confidence."

"I am entirely confident you did not kill this man and you—and possibly your friends—can figure this out. With my help. Let's go over your suspects."

"You mean now that the best one is dead?" I might have sounded a little glum.

"Let's start with him. Dwight you said his name is, right?"

"He's dead. Why start with him?"

"Because he had a good motive and perhaps that motive can be applied to someone else. Or it might reveal other possible motives."

I saw the theory, I wasn't so sure about the reality. But on the chance Kit was right, it was worth a try.

"Dwight Yagos and Bob Coble have been in competition for— excuse the expression—top dog at Torrid Avenue Dog Park for years. His motive would be that rivalry and ending it once and for all in his favor. Or, perhaps, a moment of rage, brought on by mounting anger over the years of rivalry."

I didn't buy it, though.

"What would be your theory of the crime with Dwight as the kill- er?" she asked.

"The murder part would be quite straightforward. Actually for anyone it would be. The murderer put the leash around Bob's neck, with the clip end slipped through the handle loop, and pulled it tight. We know it wouldn't have taken long for him to lose consciousness, but the killer would have had to hold it tight longer than that to kill him."

Kit grunted acknowledgement of what we'd both learned at a forensics seminar for writers. "Pretty straightforward. What's more interesting is how a killer got the leash around Bob's neck in the first place. Why would he let anyone do that?"

I expanded on her point. "And they'd have to take it away from him. Plus, why did he bring it to the park when he didn't have his dog with him?"

"That is an interesting question and it's what makes me think a woman is more likely as the murderer. Someone he trusted and had known a long time, so he'd be off-guard. Or perhaps someone he was going to instruct."

My mind flashed to Augustine Lorenson. If Bob had known about Berrie's training appointment with the woman would he have tried to break it up by meeting for a secret session ahead of time?

In a heartbeat.

And that could explain bringing the tweed lead—showing her the *proper* kind to have—and not having Trevalyn.

But why would Augustine agree to meet him during the night in the closed dog park? And why would she kill him? Could he possibly have been suing her?

I needed to check that in courthouse records in the morning.

In the meantime, there was another possibility.

"Let me tell you about Berrie Vittlow."

I filled in Aunt Kit about Berrie and Bob's history.

"Interesting. He'd crushed one of her dreams years ago—presumably to be a couple, maybe marry and have a family—and now he's threatened her current dream involving rescuing Boston terriers and being a trainer. That's a lot of emotion."

"Lawsuits are emotional, too," I countered, even though I was arguing against myself. "And there were plenty of those."

I told her about Bob's penchant for lawsuits, including Amy Kackley and his neighbors, Pamela and Jeremy Farris. Also his nit-picking offensive against Ruby, threatening her much-needed job. I ended with, "So I'll check the public record tomorrow at the courthouse."

"All good starts, Sheila. Keep going with those. But I see at least one more suspect based on what you've told me."

Would she tell me? Oh, no. Said I needed to figure it out myself.

CHAPTER THIRTY-SEVEN

I JOLTED AWAKE at the sensation of ice applied to the back of my calf.

Not ice.

But close enough.

A cold, wet collie nose that had burrowed under the covers to connect with my now goose-fleshed calf.

I reached out and felt first one ear, then all of Gracie's head as she shifted to let me pet her.

"What is it, Gracie? Are you okay? Is something wrong?"

But even as I strained to hear anything amiss in the house that might explain her action—first time she'd ever done anything like this—I realized the sheet and light blanket under my down comforter were twisted and tangled.

I also recognized the misty shreds of a dream.

I'd been dreaming about the Coble brothers who had feuded over a woman. I'd been that woman. I'd married the surviving brother … and had just realized he'd murdered my father and his brother.

Definitely not sweet dreams.

And they seemed to have disturbed not only me, but her, too.

I stroked Gracie's head again as I left out a breath. She nuzzled my hand, then moved away.

I peered through the middle-of-the-night darkness to make sense of the faint rustlings of her movements, following the tinkling sound of her tags.

She'd returned to her bed. Circled. And now settled down.

Her job done.

My job was lying awake, looking at the shifting shadows on the ceiling, wondering why the heck I'd dreamed about that and how to get it out of my head so I could get some restful sleep.

I AWAKENED THE second time to unfamiliar brightness.

I squinted at the uncurtained window. Nope, the sky wasn't blue, but it definitely was brighter than the previous days.

I looked out.

Snow. It had snowed overnight. More than a dusting we'd had the night Bob was murdered.

The sky might still be gray, but with the ground white, it was downright cheerful outside.

I was half dressed when the phone rang.

"Sheila, I'll pick you up in an hour."

"Clara? What? Why?"

"That neighbor of Bob's wants to talk to us. Well, she doesn't, really. Or she doesn't know she does. Molly says she's about to crack. Molly's wonderful at spotting things like that. So we're going to show up at her door, let her crack, and then pick up the pieces."

"But—"

"One hour. All the roads should be plowed by then, but just in case, I'll drive the SUV."

She hung up. I wouldn't have argued anyway. I'd planned to go to the courthouse first thing, but the lawsuits could wait.

I hurried Gracie through the rest of our morning routine, piled on layers, and rushed outside.

Twenty minutes into our surprise mini-winter wonderland of about three inches of snow, Gracie still reveled in it. I was less enchanted.

That was easily explained. She was playing, secured by a line hooked to her collar, but with thirty feet any direction to romp and roam. I, on the other hand, was shoveling, starting from the open garage door.

Actually, at the moment Teague's vehicle pulled up on the plowed road, I was leaning on the shovel.

"You can't leave it parked in the street. Plow might come back," I protested, when he came around the front to open the passenger door for Murphy. Teague was back in his dog park outfit, with hat pulled down, scarf pulled up, and green jacket zipped tight.

Something pecked at my memory. What—?

"It's on the street only until you're shoveled out. You know how hard it is to shovel where a car's been. Heck, even foot traffic makes it harder."

"Oh, yeah. Sure. Want to put the dogs in the back? It's fenced."

"Good idea. I already had him to the dog park, but he's still raring to go. C'mon, Murph."

Immediately, his dog bounded in the direction Teague waved. Gracie flew to his side the second I unhooked her from the line.

He walked along the edge of the driveway, rather than on it. He wore boots, in addition to the cold-weather gear I was used to from the dog park.

I sighed.

"Tired?" he asked as he returned from closing the gate behind the dogs.

"It's heavier than it looks."

"This is nothing compared to the Chicago area." He gave me that squint that was harder to meet than the most penetrating questions of seasoned interviewers. "You must have been used to this in New York."

"We had people to do shoveling." Good grief. Had the unusual brightness fried my brain? That answer had come from my author-of-*Abandon-All* life, not my fictional English teacher who unexpectedly inherited life. I scrambled to add, "At the condo where I lived. We residents didn't have to worry about any exterior maintenance. Except for paying for it."

I needed to start a spreadsheet of what I'd told to whom.

Condo. Must remember I'd said I lived in a condo.

"Huh. How about growing up around here. You had snow then, right?"

"Some. I also had older brothers. Don't blame my parents. They didn't assign tasks by gender. It was my brothers who snagged all the shoveling jobs, realizing they could make good money with a few hours of physical labor around the neighborhood. Far better per hour than lawn-mowing, which they oh, so generously left to me."

He chuckled. "Smart guys. Maybe they didn't think much of your technique."

"It's an excellent technique."

I hadn't actually been shoveling so much as pushing the snow across one side of the double driveway to the other side. It was a lot easier than trying to lift the heavy old-fashioned shovel, especially with a load of snow.

"You're only clearing one side of the driveway."

"One side works for me, since I have one car."

"When I pull in, you'll be blocked."

"You can pull out if I have to go somewhere."

It clearly bugged him to not clear the entire driveway, but he let it drop for another topic.

"You need a lighter shovel."

I agreed with that, but this behemoth, which I strongly suspected was made of iron, was what the previous owners had left in the garage, along with a rake, garbage cans, and a hose that looked older than me.

"Hey!" I protested when he took the shovel from me, not only removing my tool but my prop.

He returned to his vehicle by the same route, got a bright orange shovel from inside and came back to me.

"Here. You use this. I'll take Black Bessie, there."

"You don't have to—"

"I'll start from the street and we'll meet in the middle."

I didn't remember a lot about snow-shoveling, but did know he'd taken the harder task—where the street plows had broadcast extra layers of snow chunks at the base of the driveway—along with the metal shovel.

The bright orange shovel was a great relief to my arms and worked great as a snow-shover.

Still, Teague was faster.

I shot glances at him as we came closer and closer.

We'd all heard how Murphy showed up at his back door, shivering and soaked. And now we knew he was an ex-cop, an ex-detective, who'd left law enforcement for substitute teaching.

What had Kit said about that—a strange career path? Sure was. Yet, he'd said little about it. In fact, Teague O'Donnell said little about anything having to do with himself.

That reticence twanged a nerve somewhere inside me. Maybe it was that it takes someone keeping secrets to recognize the symptoms in someone else.

Or maybe the twang wasn't just caution.

And that posed another kind of danger.

"Why are you here, Teague?"

He looked around at me as if waiting for a punchline.

"Seriously, why are you here?"

"Shoveling snow so I can get inside to work on the shelves." His tone added a half-question and an overlay of amusement.

"Is that the only reason? Or are you also here to spy for Deputy Eckles? Or if not to spy, thinking you can solve the case yourself and get the credit? Would that get you back in law enforcement?"

He straightened and rested the shovel against his hip. "First, we don't call it spying, we call it undercover. Generally, somebody undercover does not first reveal that they've been a cop. It sort of ruins the surprise. Second, to solve the case by putting shelves in your closet and bookcases in your office, I'd have to hope evidence came visiting. And even then I might not be able to hear it over the saw and drill. Third, I'd either have to be willing to steal credit from you and, I suppose, Clara, or I'd have to prove one of you was the murderer. Fourth, it would not get me back in law enforcement."

"That was no answer. Are you spying for Eckles or do you think you can solve the case and get the credit?" I threw back at him. "Maybe get back into law enforcement. Make good on whatever reason you left."

"No."

We could have been flash frozen for all the sound or movement that followed that flat syllable. I didn't know where to take this next. And he clearly wasn't going to volunteer anything.

Who knows how long we might have stood there if Clara hadn't pulled into the bottom of the driveway then and tooted the horn.

"Go on," he ordered. "I'll finish this up and bring the dogs in when I start work inside. You and Clara go do whatever clue-hunting you've got planned. Just know this isn't a game."

"We don't—" He'd grabbed the old-fashioned shovel again and had his head down. "Fine."

I had my keys and wallet in my pocket. I didn't need anything else. I drove the blade of the orange shovel into a modest snowbank accumulated from my shoveling and headed toward Clara's SUV.

"But Sheila…"

Teague's voice stopped me, pulled my head back around to him.

"You definitely need a new shovel. This thing could anchor a boat."

CHAPTER THIRTY-EIGHT

EITHER MOLLY OR Clara had missed her calling as a fortune-teller.

We rang the doorbell of Pamela and Jeremy Farris' imposing Blue Grass Estates home, a pumpkin to my house's cantaloupe—see, I was learning from my grocery store trips.

Pamela Farris opening it, wearing a jeans and t-shirt outfit that made me think expensive, rather than comfortable.

"Hi, Pamela," Clara said. "Remember us? We met you at Molly's. We wanted to talk to you."

Pamela burst into tears.

I don't have a lot of experience with people bursting into tears when they open a door to me, but I would have expected her next move to be closing the inside door in our faces.

Instead, she fumbled at the lock on the storm door and gave it a feeble push open.

We needed no other invitation.

I handled the door, Clara handled Pamela. One arm around her shoulders, telling her not to worry, saying we'd talk, and it would all be okay. When Pamela took a step toward the starchy living room, Clara steered her, instead, to the back of the house and a couch in the family room that opened to the kitchen.

"How about some tea?"

Pamela nodded to Clara and sobbed.

I recognized that as my cue to make tea. Fortunately, there were bags of green tea in a cannister cunningly labeled "tea." Mugs were lined up on open shelving and the microwave did its magic. Heck, I even found a little round tray to carry the mugs over.

Pamela held hers like a refugee huddled around a fire, but she'd stopped crying.

About halfway through the mug, Clara said quietly, "Now, tell us what's worrying you so much."

Pamela looked up, her brown eyes immediately redrenched in tears. "What if I could have saved his life? What if I could have stopped it?"

IT TOOK TIME to calm her down again.

"How could you have done that?" I asked. See? I can be tactful, too. I didn't even bring up saving a life.

"If I'd called, if I'd only called instead of being so … so *horrible*. Staying in bed, thinking maybe he'd fallen down the stairs and hurt himself and he deserved it." She gulped. "But I never, never thought he was dead. Never."

Clara resumed consoling, also shooting me a look that said she had no idea what the woman was talking about.

I ventured, "But he hadn't, had he? Fallen down the stairs, I mean. What made you think he might have?"

"Trevalyn's barking. Barking and barking and barking. I knew something was wrong, but he was such an awful neighbor and Jeremy had said to stay away from him and Jeremy wasn't home that night, so I…" The sobs started ramping up again. "And he might not have died if it weren't for me."

A second round of tea and Clara's patience—mine had run out during the first mug of tea—pulled out the story.

She'd heard Trevalyn barking during the night. She had not called anybody about it. She felt that failure might have cost Bob Coble his life.

I doubted we completely persuaded her that calling 911 about Trevalyn barking inside would not have saved Bob. Even if it immediately raised the alarm, who would have thought to check the dog park when he didn't have his dog?

Though maybe they would have immediately spotted that stepped-on poop, done a massive dragnet for shoes newly adorned with poop, and solved the murder right then.

Or not.

I certainly didn't raise the possibility to Pamela Farris.

What I did do was ask, "What started the bad blood between Bob and you and your husband?"

It was like she lost all her bones. She slumped into a rag doll of misery.

"It's my fault. It's all my fault. Poor Jeremy. Working so hard to build a life and reputation in business, and I'm going to drag him down. I told him he should leave me. But he won't."

"How is it your fault?"

"My ... my daddy's a criminal. He's in prison. Again." She said a name that meant nothing to me, but clearly did to Clara. She mouthed *Later* to me. "I can't run away from that name, even though I'm now a Farris, and it will besmirch Jeremy's name and reputation."

I cut through the drama with another question. "How did Bob find out?"

"He went through our mail. He came up to the door, holding it out to me one day with this ... this *smile* saying he'd wanted to save me the trouble. And then he said something about family and I thought he was hinting around about when we were going to have another baby, but when I saw the letter Daddy had written from prison in the pile, I knew...

"After that, he was real mean. Thought he could boss me and Jeremy around, telling us what to plant in our yard and wanting us to kill the dandelions with chemicals and all sorts of things. But Jeremy wouldn't and it got worse and worse and then the lawsuit and I knew it would all come out in court, like it did for my poor mama, sitting there hearing the *horrible* things Daddy had done—*twice*! At least now she doesn't believe him anymore, but it was so *awful* for her.

"And I was in bed that night thinking about all those things and I heard Trevalyn barking and I was just *evil* thinking those things and never calling anybody."

"But we've been over that," Clara said. "You couldn't have saved Bob. You have to stop tormenting yourself about that."

"At the very least I could have spared Trevalyn that miserable time alone."

"Well, that's true," Clara said.

Pamela burst into tears again.

CHAPTER THIRTY-NINE

"THERE'S NO WAY on earth that poor girl killed Bob," Clara declared as we neared my house.

She'd told me first that she wouldn't be surprised if a new little Farris joined the neighborhood in seven or eight months, suspecting hormones fueled Pamela's waterworks.

Then she filled me in that Pamela's father had been a state legislator until he was caught with his pants down—literally—and his pockets stuffed with illicit cash—proverbially. He came out of prison, having found Jesus, redemption, and absolute proof that evolution did not exist, he proclaimed, and set up as a preacher, who needed folks' generous donations to support his mission in sharing what he'd learned. Two years later it was Act Two. He was now back in prison.

"Unless she's a really good actress," I told Clara.

"*Oh.*"

"Watch out, Clara. Amy's backing out of her driveway."

She had been, but then she pulled back in, perhaps deciding not to risk the roads until a distracted Clara parked.

"Sheila, you think Pamela could have—?"

"I don't know. But she did have motive. We have nothing to go on except what she told us. Not only her actions that night, but Jeremy's. What if he thought Bob could have ruined them? Where exactly was he that night? And can he prove it?"

"Oh, those are all such great questions." She pulled into my now-cleared driveway behind Teague's vehicle. "But before we discuss them, I have to run into your house. All that tea…"

"Go right ahead." I'd wisely used the facilities at Pamela Farris' house in an entirely anonymous powder room that told me nothing, even when I looked in the cabinet and under the sink.

As I started to follow Clara in, I heard my name.

I looked around and Amy Kackley was walking diagonally across the street.

"Sorry. Clara got a little distracted. Hope it didn't scare you."

"What? No. That was fine. I … I wanted to talk to you."

She said the words with no joy in her heart. Amy wasn't the bursting into tears type, but if she had been, I'd have been experiencing déjà vu, judging by that tone.

"Yes?" Okay, I could have been more encouraging. But what if my assessment of Amy's tearfulness quotient was wrong. I would deal with another outburst if I had to, but I didn't have to beg for it.

Amy's jaw moved like she was unclenching her teeth.

"I saw Dwight."

"What? When?"

"There at the dog park after Bob's body was found. For a minute, barely even that. He got out of his van and our eyes met for an instant—I know he saw me—and then he got back in and he left. He looked … He looked awful. Just awful. I haven't told anybody.

"But now he's dead. People are saying he must have killed himself right after killing Bob, but I know that's not right. And the rumors about his scarf … He was wearing it. Like always. His hat and the scarf and the jacket with the hood pulled up. But he looked like I'd never seen him look before."

She wasn't crying, but she trembled.

North Bend County couldn't possibly have two great actors, could it?

I took hold of her arms and looked into her eyes. "You have to go to the sheriff's department, Amy. Right now. Ask for Deputy Eckles or Deputy Hensen. Don't leave until you've told one of them this. Do you understand?"

A single nod.

"Do you want me to go with you?"

A sideways jerk of her head.

"Get Donna to go with you?

A repeat.

She parted her lips, drew in a breath. "I knew I had to, but I needed someone to say it. When I saw you with Clara … I still don't think Dwight did this. And I can't find it in me to be crying for Bob Coble. But a person has to tell the truth, not try to massage it to their liking. I'm going now."

She pivoted, my hands falling away from her. She took the direct path to her vehicle.

I stood there, watching, as she backed out and went the opposite direction from the library, taking the route to the sheriff's department.

Damn. I'd missed asking her what rumors about Dwight's scarf.

AS I TURNED to go into the house, I received a text from Kit.

Prelim shows Teague O'Donnell legit. More to come. Diving into deadline.

Kit on deadline?

The entire globe could be packed up and transported to Saturn and Kit wouldn't notice when she was on deadline.

This was bad.

I'd lost my murder sounding board, my guru, my consultant.

I'd also lost the buffer between me and my mother, who knew I'd been around a murder, and my father, who would know as soon as Mom cracked, which she would do sooner without Kit's reassurance.

Bad, bad, bad.

I FOUND CLARA curled up on the loveseat in my office, watching Teague mark out measurements for the bookshelves there. From the smell, he'd started painting the shoe shelves in the other room.

"I was telling him about Pamela," she said cheerfully.

Behind his back, I gave her a sharp we-talked-about-this glare.

She returned a What?-I-checked-him-out-and-he's-really-a-cop look.

I gave her a doesn't-mean-we-have-to-blab-everything frown.

She tilted her head for a Cop!-Detective!-he-might-be-able-to-help-us response.

I gave up. At least for now.

I told them about my encounter with Amy.

A sentence in, Teague turned, fat pencil and measuring tape still in hand.

"That's sure interesting," Clara said, "but does it change anything?"

"Okay, I don't want you two to get all excited about this, because it's not something I was told outright—Hell, I have no idea why I'm telling you now. But—"

"You know you'll be the next to die if you don't tell us," I inserted.

His eyes lit up. "Are you threatening me?"

"No. Informing you about what happens next in all the books and movies so you can make a good decision. The person with the knowledge that would solve everything gets killed before he's smart enough to share it."

"She's right," Clara said immediately. "You better tell us right away. It's the only way to save your life."

"I don't doubt that for a moment." His mouth quirked. "Trouble with your theory is that more people than me know this. It's gotten around. In fact, I heard most of it when I was out at the big box store because the hardware store here in town is closed on Sundays. Still, remember, this is something I gathered from a few comments. I could be totally wrong, have put things together the wrong way or—"

"For Pete's sake, just tell us."

I stifled a giggle at Clara's outburst, but Teague appeared taken aback.

"The leash might not have been the murder weapon."

CHAPTER FORTY

"WHAT?"

My one-syllable question covered two octaves, possibly three. Clara looked stunned.

"There's the possibility the leash wasn't the murder weapon," he repeated.

"We heard you, but—"

"Why? How?" Clara demanded. "We saw it around his neck. Tight around his neck."

"The leash was definitely around his neck, but the ME—medical examiner—might have found indications something else was used first, then the leash put on, either to finish the job or maybe to mask the first thing used."

"What was the first thing used?"

"No way I could say for sure."

Clara and I stared at him.

"Okay, okay, it's being talked about at the big box store, so I suppose it can't hurt ... Possibly a blow. Or something else used to strangle him. The ME might have found blue and white fibers."

"Blue and wh—Dwight's UK scarf," Clara cried. Then the pitch of her cry changed. "And then he put it back around his neck and wore it to the dog park the next day? No wonder Amy said he looked so awful."

I zeroed in on Teague. "The ME *might have* found blue and white fibers?"

He carefully put down pencil and measuring tape, then turned back to us and shrugged. "I haven't talked to the ME directly, so I don't know for sure. I don't even know who did talk to the ME. It's like a game of telephone. Or a couple games of telephone, one line passing down one bit of information and a second another bit of information, then they get put together. It's not evidence, much less anything that would stand up in court."

"Which line came at the big box store?"

"The blue and white. Couldn't believe it was being talked about like that."

"So the ME finding that something other than Bob's leash actually killed him, that came to you from a more reliable game of telephone?"

"Maybe." It was as far as he'd go.

"How does this—. How *might* this," I conceded under his frown as I sat behind my desk, "change how we look at our suspects?"

"It would make Dwight a lot more likely—which would break his grandmother's heart if it's not already broken because he's dead," Clara said.

"Good point. If it wasn't Dwight's UK scarf, how hard a blow to the neck are we talking about?"

Teague shrugged again. "Don't know for sure. Bob was a pretty slight guy. If the victim was somebody the size of Dwight, a possible blow to the neck would eliminate lots of people because they couldn't reach."

"Ruby would have a hard time reaching even with Bob. I don't see how she could have killed him with a blow, either. Not unless she knows martial arts or something."

Clara shook her head. "Never heard of her or Amy Kackley knowing that sort of thing, though Amy's at least several inches taller than Ruby, so there's that."

"Even without training, it's hard but not entirely impossible. Especially with adrenaline going."

Teague, leaning against the window frame, gave me a bemused look. "Voice of experience?"

"All those mysteries she's read," Clara said.

I ignored that detour. "Berrie could reach, she's nearly Bob's height."

"So could Pamela and Jeremy Farris. The neighbors of Bob I told you about," Clara said to Teague. Then she sighed. "This doesn't get us very far."

"No, but let's keep going. If the murderer killed him with a blow to the neck, why put the leash on?"

"Don't get too caught up in the idea of a blow," Teague said. "It's only a possibility."

Clara sat up from her morose slump, ignoring him and going back to what I'd said. "Right. Why put the leash on? It sure couldn't pass as an accident after that. Not if the UK scarf was used first then swapped out, either. But if it was a blow to the neck and they didn't use the leash, it might never have been investigated—"

"A guy found dead in the dog park—it was always going to be investigated," Teague objected.

"Okay, but the leash immediately made everybody think it was murder."

"Unless it was a sex game."

"*Bob?*" Clara demanded. "No way."

"You'd be surprised," Teague muttered.

Clara and I exchanged a look. We weren't asking him to explain that. Not now, anyway.

"Back to Clara's point that it makes everybody think murder. Who would benefit from that?"

"Somebody we'd never suspect," Clara said promptly.

"Great. Except who? It's not like there's somebody he's been close to whom we haven't suspected." I was proud of that whom. It was what an English teacher would say. I hoped Teague was paying attention.

"Because he hasn't been close to anybody."

"That brings up a good point. I wonder who inherits?"

"Oh, that's a great point." Clara looked impressed.

Actually, I should have thought of it long ago. It was basic. "Teague, have you heard anything from your official sources?"

"I don't have any sources. Especially not official sources." He said it so firmly it made me wonder … But he wasn't budging.

"I'll find out what the rumor mill says about that. I haven't heard anything yet, but sometimes a little priming works wonders."

"Great, Clara. I still want to check the suits."

Teague cleared his throat. "One thing you haven't explored is what Clara said at the beginning—this makes Dwight more likely. His size and strength, he could have hit Bob out of anger or even wrapped the scarf around his neck, not trying to kill him. But he did. Then Dwight realized Bob was dead and panicked. He put Bob's leash around his neck to throw off suspicion."

"It didn't throw off suspicion at all."

"He couldn't have known that. Especially not in a panic. When he did realize it, he committed suicide."

"Wait a minute," I said slowly. "We were talking before about why the dog park and why the leash. What if it was because the murder *wasn't* about the dog park, but the murderer wanted to make it look like it was?"

"You do know most murders are pretty straight forward, don't you?" Teague asked. "The most likely guy is the most likely because they usually do it. That's what I was saying about Dwight."

"Maybe in your world," Clara said dismissively, "but those are the easy ones. Go on, Sheila, what were you saying?"

"It would still be about Bob, since he's the one who died. Think about Bob, what kind of person he was."

"You mean he liked secrets?" Clara asked.

"Oh, yes, he definitely liked secrets. Look at how he called collie rescue on me."

"He what?" Teague asked.

I explained succinctly. "And, yes," I said to his expression, "Someone might think that gave me a motive to kill Bob. But not a motive to kill Dwight."

"Cover your tracks," he said immediately. "Have a fall guy."

Clara groaned. "This is all my fault. I'm sorry. I'm so sorry, Sheila. If I'd known that information came from Bob, I'd have told them he wasn't reliable. When I did talk to them about you, I swear it was all wonderful. After seeing you with Gracie—"

"I know. Stop apologizing. It's not the most comfortable thing to know I was checked out, but I'd rather that happen ten times over if it means they catch one bad adopter. As for Bob, you couldn't have known he was the source. But it's more than his liking secrets. Or something *beyond* that. I can't quite … Ah…" I held up my index finger. The mildest, most modest of *Eurekas*. "He didn't only like knowing secrets about people, he used what he knew."

"What do you mean?"

I was sorting that out myself as words came out of my mouth. "Some people are satisfied once they know the secret. That satisfies a need for power. But Bob Coble went beyond that. He *used* the power, the leverage the secret gave him. He wasn't satisfied with only knowing. He wanted it to accomplish something for him. He used rules as weapons, that's what Amy said. Wouldn't he have used secrets the same way? Rosie, the woman at bunco who'd been his neighbor said he looked through their mail, like he did with Pamela and Jeremy Farris. Looking for a secret, a weapon."

"Oh. Like his cracks to me that last day at the dog park."

"Cracks?"

"About knowing why I was hanging around with you. He'd guessed somehow that I was the one checking on you for collie rescue and he was warning me not to get in his way or he'd blab to you." She gusted out a sigh. "And I was too much of a wimp to tell you the truth and tell him to go jump in the creek."

I dragged up the exchange from my memory. "You're right. You're exactly right. That's the other element. He found out people's secrets, then he let them know he knew it. Because otherwise it wasn't a weapon."

Boy, if he'd known my real secret … Thank heavens he'd fixated on my disregarding his dog training advice and hadn't dug into my past fifteen years.

On the other hand, if Teague O'Donnell began digging into my past, I doubted he'd use what he learned as weapons. That was the good news. The bad news was he wouldn't be satisfied with the first secret he came upon.

I shivered.

"It is horrible," Clara said, interpreting my shiver in line with our conversation. "He was so nasty."

"He came up against someone even nastier."

CHAPTER FORTY-ONE

I SHOULD HAVE gone to the courthouse to look up those lawsuits.

Clara should have gone home and fixed something wonderful for dinner for her wonderful and understanding husband.

Teague should have stayed and worked on my shelves.

Actually, Teague did do that.

But Clara and I went to the dog park. Yes, we took our dogs.

They were the whole reason to go.

Despite our best efforts to give them some exercise, neither one had been worn out the past several days, which meant they had plenty of reserves in their tanks. I wasn't sure about LuLu, but I could practically see Gracie vibrating.

We would let them blow out their physical cobwebs, while we blew out our mental cobwebs.

Teague declined to leave his worksite to bring his dog. Clara even volunteered to bring Murphy with us.

Hearing that name got Gracie's immediate attention, but neither her adorableness in recognizing the name nor Clara's offer swayed Teague.

And how much could I complain about his staying, considering the work he was doing?

But he did not need to hit us with the parting shot of, "You really think you're going to put this all together by the two of you standing around at the dog park?"

✦　✦　✦　✦

TURNED OUT, HE was right about the standing. Not even Clara and I were going to sit in the snow.

He was wrong about the two of us.

Berrie was in the small dog enclosure we'd all used yesterday with the Bostons. Donna, with her golden, Hattie, and a pair of other Sane Middles and their dogs were in the smaller large-dog enclosure, now opened, while the others remained marked off with police tape.

Marcus had to adjust his show for the new venue, but worked in his whole routine when I reached the vestibule.

Clara and I let our dogs go, then I stepped off the concrete into the moderately pristine snow.

Then I stopped, in sync with Marcus turning off. "Let's talk to Donna."

I asked if I could have a word and led her away from her friends.

"Amy called me on the way to the sheriff's department," Donna said when we were out of earshot. "I knew something has been bothering her. But she held it in. I'm glad you told her to go."

I stifled an urge to say she'd probably saved herself from being Next to Die by telling me, with Donna as a backup.

Clara would have gotten it, but not Donna.

"Donna, I'd like you to listen to what happened the day Dwight and Bob fought, the day before Bob was murdered. This—"

"I heard all about what happened that day."

"Not from us. And we were among the few who were here." I looked at Clara. "Stop me if I get anything wrong or leave anything out."

I started with the first argument we'd heard between them that day, the one where Bob sneered at Dwight's control of Skeeter. I gave every detail I could think of, using their exact words when I remembered them. The dogs milling around, Dwight's use of a curse word, the brevity of the conflict, Dwight being the one to walk away, with Skeeter trailing behind.

Donna made no comment and Clara had nothing to add, so I moved on to the second round. When I finished that, I looked at Clara.

"The only thing I'd add is Dwight peeled out of the parking lot. I remember seeing his little SUV rock from side to side as he made the turn."

Donna looked at her sharply. "Did it?"

"Yes," I confirmed.

"I thought Skeeter must have had a rocky ride," Clara added.

"Hmm." Donna looked down at the toes of her boots.

Clara and I looked at her, then at each other. Clara raised her brows.

Another few minutes of silence.

I couldn't take it any longer. "Anything strike you about that, Donna?"

"Yes. Skeeter."

CHAPTER FORTY-TWO

"Skeeter?"

"From everything I'd heard before, it was clear Dwight was in a state. But from how you describe it, Skeeter was in a state, too."

"What do you mean?"

"You said he looked up at Bob. Like he was going to attack? Like he hated him?"

"No. Not at all."

With a glance, I invited Clara to comment. She frowned. "More like … asking him something."

"Ah. Whatever was wrong with Dwight—and clearly there was something wrong. Not just the squabbling with Bob going too physical, but swearing and rocketing out of the lot in a way sure to be hard on Skeeter…?" She shook her head. "Definitely something wrong with Dwight. So wrong, it was also making his relationship with Skeeter all wrong, too."

Clara looked as confused as I felt.

Donna propped her hands on her hips. "Skeeter and Dwight are bonded, right? Skeeter knows to look to Dwight for everything—food, treats, water, play, cues about how to act, what's a danger, and who's a friend. And who's not. Skeeter knows Bob is not a danger, but also isn't a friend. Then something weird happens. The angry words he's used to become more than words. And what does he do? He looks at Bob—*Bob!*—and he's slow to follow Dwight."

She gestured to the other two Sane Middles who were waving to her, indicating it was time to leave.

"I've gotta go now, but if you can figure out some way to question Skeeter, I think you'd learn a lot."

She was still laughing at her own joke as she closed the main gate behind her.

Clara and I stared at each other.

Finally, I said, "She didn't say a word about Trevalyn's reactions."

"That's because he acted normally."

"He did, didn't he?"

Memories raced on fast forward.

"Oh, my God, he did." I grabbed Clara's arm. "I've got it. I think I've got it."

…if you knew half as much about dogs as you're pretending to…

You are not fit to have responsibility for a dog…

My dream from last night … two men fighting over one woman.

But…

"*Maybe* I've got it."

"What? What do you think?" Clara demanded.

I held up a finger, ordering her to wait as I dug my phone out of an inner pocket—since the day we'd found Bob, I kept it on me, not in my car.

"Teague? It's Sheila." I said when he answered.

"Teague?" Clara muttered, frowning at me.

"I'm putting you on speaker phone. Clara's here, too. Remember that night at the grocery store?"

"What about it?"

"When you came up behind me and tried to scare the bejabbers out of me—"

"I did not. I said hello. You jumped a mile and threw onions all around."

"Why did you throw onions?" Clara asked me.

"I didn't and that is not at all what happened—" I sucked in a breath and waved one hand as if erasing a dry board.

"That doesn't matter now. What matters is how did you know it was me, Teague?"

"What do you mean how did I know it was you? I recognized

you."

"How? I had my back to you."

I was sure—pretty sure—I knew. But I didn't want to say more. I needed him to say it. If my crazy idea wasn't so crazy after all I definitely needed him to say this.

He paused, but I thought it was in concentration, rather than hesitation. "I recognized… Yeah. I saw your coat from the back and knew it was you."

"Ahhhh."

"What?" Clara demanded.

"That's how I recognized you, too. Without all your dog park gear, I didn't know it was you, but I saw the green jacket and *that* I knew. It's how we *do* recognize each other at the park in this weather. All wrapped up, faces mostly covered, recognition depends so much on the coat or jacket or *scarf*."

"The scarf," they both repeated.

"Yes. The scarf. Dwight's scarf. That's what we recognized. If we saw anyone wearing that scarf, along with the UK jacket, the UK hat, we might take it for granted that it was Dwight Yagos, especially if the person was about the right size and shape."

"And had Skeeter with him," Clara murmured.

I grabbed her arm." Exactly. That's brilliant, Clara."

"Is it?"

"It is. Because if he didn't have Skeeter at the dog park, we wouldn't think it was Dwight, even with the scarf. The dog without the scarf, sure. We'd think he'd forgotten the scarf. Well, we might also think the universe had started rotating the opposite way, but still, the point holds. Skeeter was the essential. The scarf without the dog? Unthinkable."

Teague sounded strained. "Let me get this straight. Are you saying—"

"Sorry. Gotta go." I handed Clara my phone and stalked off toward the far corner of the enclosure.

I needed quiet. Just for a moment.

There was something … something…

I was running back scenes and conversations. From the past several days, from earlier…

Trying to make them a whole instead of snippets.

Then the *something* became a hand waving in front of my face.

"Have you heard a thing I said?" Clara demanded.

"No. I was thinking. Is Teague still on the line?"

"No. He said some bad words, then hung up. What were you thinking about?"

I took my phone, clicked it off, dropped it in my outer pocket, and stared at our dogs locked in mock battle over a mouthful of snow. "Dogs."

She sniffed. "I suppose this is the place to do it."

"Have you ever noticed, Clara, how the dogs will wrestle and tussle like it's the most serious battle in the world? And then they just stop."

"Well, yeah. We've only talked about that a hundred times. What's gotten into you, Sheila?"

But I was too deep into the thought rattling its chains to answer her question. I had my own. "Why do you think that is, Clara?"

"How would I know? It's … Okay, okay, I'll humor you. Say it's because they have some secret language we don't know, and they're communicating and somebody's said, let's knock off on the count of three."

I tipped my head, slanting the canine picture before me.

"So a secret language could also work when they're fighting? I mean when a dog takes serious exception to another."

"No." Clara's rare impatience snipped the ends of the words. "Because they're friends. And they're playing."

I straightened my head, turning to Clara. "What if they're not friends but they're still playing. Play-acting and they both know it. So they know exactly when to stop. That's it, Clara. That's it. That changes everything."

"What's it? What changes—?"

"How many times did you see Bob and Dwight act out that scene? The big, dramatic argument. The raised voices. The accusations of not knowing how to train a dog."

"A dozen."

Ah, Clara the optimist.

"Clara, I've seen it a dozen and a half times and I've only been here a month."

She grimaced. "You're right. Say, twelve times a month for at least six years. That's—"

"A lot. And every time they played out that scene, even with variations, they always knew when to stop. Where to stop. So they didn't go past the line that wouldn't let them ever have the play-acting fight again because they'd gone too far in the previous one."

"But … But…"

"Just like the dogs," I added, having the slightest suspicion I might not be crystal clear in my explanation. "They might growl and fuss at each other, but there's a line they don't pass. Don't you see? C'mon, get your stuff. Get LuLu. Gracie, come."

Clara took the leash I handed her. "Except the dogs don't always follow the secret language. Remember when that mix picked up the Scottie, who didn't belong in the big dog area, and started to shake him—

"*Exactly!*" I whirled on her triumphantly. She jumped back. "And what did the other dogs do?"

"They barked at him—Gracie most of all—and he immediately dropped the Scottie."

"Right. And then the mix rolled over to expose his belly, apologizing. And order was restored." Though Gracie kept a closer eye on that mix, I'd noticed. She took her role as dog park referee seriously.

I patted her on the head after hooking her leash to her collar. We all started toward the gate.

"I'm sorry, Sheila, but I don't see how this applies to Bob and Dwight. Because they didn't know when to stop, even when we were telling them to. Dwight would have hit Bob if Teague hadn't been here."

"*Exactly!*"

"I wish you'd stop saying that as if it explained everything, when I have no idea what you mean."

"Why would Bob and Dwight not know when to stop when they *had* stopped all those other times?"

"You're going to make me figure this out? Why not just tell me?"

"That's not fun." Another trick I'd learned from Kit.

She groaned. "This is like when Ned insists on explaining carburetors or something to me on the car. I appreciate his knowing about them and working on them. But I just want the darned thing to run. Fine, fine. Okay. Bob and Dwight would not know when to stop this time when they had all those other times because ... one of them was drunk or on drugs. Because one of them was sick. Because—" She opened her eyes wider. "—one of them had something bad happen in his life and was beside himself. But—"

"Hold up there. What do those three possibilities you mentioned have in common?"

"Sheila."

"Okay, okay. You could say all three were another way of saying one of them wasn't himself. In fact, you *did* say. You said exactly that. *He's not himself today*."

"Oh-kay." She made it two long you-still-sound-crazy-to-me syllables.

"Because he *wasn't* himself."

CHAPTER FORTY-THREE

WE HAD TO get out the main gate before Marcus stopped his carrying on … with Berrie pretending she didn't hear a thing.

By the frown pleating her forehead, Clara was thinking hard. "I don't … Just tell me. Who murdered Bob?"

"Dwight did it. Dwight killed Bob."

"Really? Okay, okay, I won't argue. But then who killed Dwight?"

"Dwight did that, too."

"What are you talking about?"

She stopped dead, so I stopped, too.

"Two Dwights. That's what I'm talking about. The one we knew and another one."

"A secret twin?" Her eyes lit up.

"No, no. Cousins who look a lot alike. Remember the photo in Mrs. Yagos' room? Remember her saying dark and light and hard to tell apart. I thought she meant the girls, the one with the dyed blonde hair and the other with dark hair. But what if she meant Dwight and the cousin who explored that creek as kids? All those family members look so much alike. Bundle them up, put a UK hat, UK jacket, UK scarf—especially the scarf—on almost any of them and they'd look enough like Dwight—"

"Oh, my God, you're saying it wasn't Dwight here at the dog park that day? That's what you were getting at with Teague? About how he recognized you at the grocery store? How you recognized him."

"Exactly. We recognize each other by our clothes. We're so wrapped up out here, you can hardly see us anyway. He'd probably already killed Dwight. Oh. Yes, yes, yes. The neighbor. Dwight's neighbor said Dwight had a visitor from out of town, but he hadn't seen the visitor. He probably did, but thought it was Dwight. We saw someone who looked like Dwight. And everyone accepted that. Everyone except Bob. That's why he had to die. C'mon. Let's go. We have to get to the sheriff's office."

"I'm still not sure I understand everything you're saying about Bob and Dwight and not-Dwight," Clara said plaintively as we passed Berrie's Boston terrier plastered vehicle to cross two open spots before Clara's SUV.

"That's okay. We'll tell Deputy Eckles and it'll get clearer. Do you have your keys? I'll drive."

There was another vehicle, past her big SUV. It looked like—.

"Yes, but—"

"Hand them over, lady. The keys. Right now."

CHAPTER FORTY-FOUR

IN THAT FIRST second my thought was, Really? *We're getting car-jacked for Clara's dog-scented and -decorated SUV?*

Nope. We were being held at gunpoint by not-Dwight.

And the vehicle on the far side of Clara's was Dwight's.

I wasted time with a few internalized swear words and self-recriminations. Why hadn't I checked the lot first? True, his vehicle tucked in behind Clara's big one, but if I'd looked closely, wouldn't I have seen it? We could have called the sheriff's department from the enclosure. Heck, we could have climbed the fence, forded the creek, and run to the sheriff's department if we'd had to.

The next couple of ticks I wasted on optimism.

Berrie.

Another mental swear word.

Never mind.

But wouldn't someone see us from the road? Two, then three, then five cars went by. Surely someone would notice two women and two dogs being held at gunpoint.

Or not, since the vehicles—Clara's and Dwight's—blocked their line of sight … if they were looking this way at all. And, in all fairness, her vehicle blocked Berrie's line of sight, too.

I didn't want my last thoughts to be unfair.

I spun around and looked into the face of the man who was not Dwight.

Gracie growled. I tightened her leash almost to the collar, trying to get her behind me. She twisted and curled, trying to stay in front of me.

"I've called 911. They're listening right now. They'll be here any second."

"Right," he scoffed. "Give me your phone."

My heart jumped up. If I could reach in and hit 911 while pretending to fish for the phone…

But I needed to keep him thinking about something else.

"You're Dwight's cousin, aren't you? What's your name?"

He smirked. "Guess it doesn't matter if you know, considering where you're going. Erwin."

"You do look a lot like Dwight. But did you really think you could pass for him while taking all your grandmother's money through the power of attorney?"

Clara cut me a look, but I concentrated on the non-Dwight. Erwin.

"Old lady's gaga. Besides, I'd've been out of here fast. And the money would've all been moved before anybody knew what was happening."

"But when you came here to the park with Skeeter—Why did you come here—? Oh? Dress rehearsal before you went to see your grandmother, wasn't it? But Bob figured out you weren't Dwight." The tip of my finger found the edge of the phone. It had slid down sideways in my pocket. "That must've been a shock. He ruined your plan."

"I adapted. Think on my feet. Plan B. The old lady wasn't going to sign a new will—"

"Because she sensed you weren't Dwight," Clara flung at him. "So you weren't going to be able to step into his life and take all her money."

A grating hack passed for a laugh. "Fine with me. I get a big share in the old will. And you think that Bob guy was so smart? He called Dwight's phone to warn him, all superior. When he realized it was me, the jackass started lecturing how I didn't know anything about dogs. I acted all humble and said I wanted to learn and he fell for it. But I said it had to be in secret, at night, the back way, not to hurt Dwight's feelings. He'd've gone to the moon to show up Dwight. I was waiting, inside. Told him to come over the fence. He started climbing, bitching the whole way, until at the top, he asked where the dog was. I hooked him with that stupid scarf of Dwight's, dragged him down, and finished it."

My fingers found the front of the phone, but I had to unlock it. I prayed I was touching the right spots.

"You stepped in dog crap, didn't you?"

"What if I did?" His eyes narrowed.

"They can test it. Prove it was you." Oops. Probably not a topic to keep him entertained. "But why use Trevalyn's lead—?"

"Putting that guy's fancy dog leash around his neck was just funny. Besides, might've needed the scarf for more Dwight-playing. That Bob guy said he hadn't told anybody about me, but I figured he'd blabbed to one of you. Showing off. Couldn't know which one, so you'll all go. If they hadn't closed the damned park, I could've gotten it done a lot sooner and been outta here."

Was that a faint beep I'd heard of the phone unlocking?

"Whose fault is it they closed the Torrid Avenue Dog Park?" Clara demanded.

I wanted to kick her.

Except he didn't get angrier. He grew smug. "We'll see who's bright. It's sure not Dwight, because he's dead. Taking his phone, that was smart. That's how I got that old guy. That's how I knew you'd found him. It started going off like crazy. Hustled out here and saw cops all over. Couldn't stick around to find out who you were or tail you then. Every damned body knew Dwight. Patience. Knew I'd get another chance. When I've cleaned up you three, I'll disappear for good. Until Gran croaks and I get my share—can't be long now."

"People will recognize you."

"You think I'd come back *here*? They'll send the money to me when she goes. I cleaned out Dwight so I can coast until the big payday." He turned the gun on Clara, but spoke to me. "Enough. Give me the phone or she gets it."

Slowly, I pulled the phone out. I'd unlocked it, but no more.

He glanced at the screen and laughed. "You didn't call the cops, you stupid—"

"Hey," Clara objected. Really, she was going to correct his bad language at this moment?

He tapped the screen. "Here's the last number you called. You didn't call 911, you idiot."

"No, she didn't."

For a second, I had no idea where the voice came from.

I didn't have one of those it might be God speaking from on-high moments. First, it didn't sound on-high. Second, I'd never heard of God speaking from behind a PortaPotty.

Also, it sounded familiar.

"Who——?" Erwin spun around.

I shoved Clara, hard, pushing her behind her SUV, and went sideways to follow, with both dogs dragged along with us.

It wasn't as much protection from a bullet as, oh, say, a tank, but it was better than a bunch of air.

"She *did* call a cop, though," the familiar voice finished. Teague O'Donnell. And then came the sound of sirens approaching. "And I called 911. Drop your weapon."

Erwin shot the PortaPotty.

Clara and I screamed.

Gracie charged back toward Erwin, yanking her leash free. LuLu followed.

So did I. Clara, from behind, pulled my jacket, but I couldn't tell if she was trying to tug me back or get past me.

"Come out or the dog gets it," Erwin shouted.

I skidded to a stop. He had LuLu's collar. He was trying to keep his gun on her, Gracie, me, the SUV, Clara, and the PortaPotty.

Then Murphy came flying around the other side of the PortaPotty, leaping toward the man's arm.

He twisted away. But that twisted his wrist right into the grip of Gracie's teeth as she leapt up.

He was screaming as he dropped the gun.

And that was before I kneed him and Clara stomped his instep.

He stopped when Teague hit him.

With lights and sirens, sheriff's department vehicles streamed into the dog park lot.

EPILOGUE

Clara and I sat on weatherproof pads, under a shared weatherproof blanket, watching our dogs at the otherwise deserted Torrid Avenue Dog Park.

It was precipitating.

Rain? Ice? Sleet? Snow? Freezing rain? Take your pick.

It was the end of February in North Bend County, Kentucky.

"I still say you shouldn't have given me all the credit with Deputy Eckles," Clara said.

"My pleasure." Truly, truly, my pleasure. "You did a great job on that interview yesterday with the Cincy TV station. Loved the plug at the end for rescue and shelter dogs."

We'd been to see Mrs. Yagos three more times, bringing new smelly stuff along. She wanted us to bring Gracie and LuLu. Carolyn had thoughts on getting past Geraldine that needed refining.

The murders remained a prime topic with us, but each day a little less.

"Thanks. I'm getting less nervous, so that's good. Of course, Berrie is all over the place, talking about her trauma and all that nonsense. She wasn't anywhere near the bullets. Teague won't even let the sheriff's department give out his name, much less do interviews."

He'd called 911 as he left my house for the dog park. He had no idea the non-Dwight was there, but picked up enough to be pretty sure I'd made a breakthrough.

And, he'd told us more than once, he didn't want me to be the next one killed because I hadn't told anybody what I knew. Or Clara and me, because I'd told only her.

When he saw the vehicle he recognized as Dwight's—cop training, I guess—he parked on the road and he and Murphy came across fields, prepared to jump him at Dwight's vehicle. When he realized we were on the other side of Clara's SUV, he got behind the only cover available—the PortaPotty.

"You know what I realized during that interview?" Clara asked me now. "I realized Bob figured it out first. He was the first one to recognize Erwin wasn't Dwight. He'd've liked that. Of course, *he* wasn't distracted by a murder, but, still, that was pretty impressive."

I nodded. "You're right. It makes sense, too. Bob liked secrets and liked using them as weapons. So he was on the lookout for secrets. Plus, what had been the most important relationship in his life these past years? Dwight."

"*Dwight?*"

"Yes. As an antagonist. The antagonist who defined Bob. Bob and Dwight paid closer attention to each other than anyone else. They had to. How else could they gripe about each other? How else could they point out flaws in what the other one did?"

"I see that. I do. He watched Dwight all the time, looking for anything he could criticize or mock. You're right. Who better to spot that it wasn't Dwight?"

"Skeeter," I said.

"Skeeter? *Oh.*"

"Exactly. Remember what Donna said. That it wasn't like Skeeter not to be right at Dwight's side, ready to mix it up. But we saw how he was that day with the non-Dwight and—Well, how could you describe Skeeter's reaction?"

"Confused," she said promptly. "He knew it wasn't Dwight, but it was someone who looked and sounded like Dwight, wearing Dwight's clothes. And according to that neighbor, Erwin had been staying with them for several days before—*Oh.*" I was growing fond of her little *Oh*s of discovery. "He must have killed Dwight away from Skeeter, because Skeeter would have known and reacted very differently to him. Erwin. The non-Dwight."

"Good point, Clara."

Deputy Eckles and the rest of the department had all that to sort out. Or to get Erwin to tell them.

She sighed. "This has all been more exciting than I ever expected. Challenging and brain-stretching. But in another way, so sad. Bob dead. Dwight dead. And feeling suspicious of people you know and like."

I see at least one more suspect based on what you've told me.

Clara.

Clara had been Great-Aunt Kit's *other suspect.*

I could see it from Kit's perspective, knowing Clara only as a collection of traits. Including her great interest in the case. Murderers did sometimes insert themselves in an investigation.

I could also see why I'd missed—or dismissed—the possibility.

Even in my initial hurt, anger, and mostly fear about her reporting to collie rescue, I'd never considered her a murder suspect.

As if she'd caught a whisper of my thoughts, she said, "I really am sorry for spying on you and Gracie."

"Don't be. I'd rather have people looking out for dogs than not. Especially someone like you—who agrees so much with me about how to treat them."

She chuckled. "Who knows how long it might have taken us to start talking if collie rescue hadn't asked me to check on you. We might not have become friends for ages."

I shook my head. "It was a sure thing. Gracie and LuLu would have seen to it. Along with the third musketeer."

We didn't dare say Murphy's name for fear Gracie and LuLu would hear it.

Murphy and Gracie had been examined by three dog experts the week after the event to be sure their defense of us didn't indicate aggressive tendencies. They all agreed the dogs were safe for society.

Good thing. I'm not sure what Clara would have done to those experts if they hadn't. I am sure what I would have done.

"We need Teague's key," Clara said.

"*What?*"

"So we can get you-know-who—" I swear Gracie lifted her head at that pseudonym for Murphy. "—and bring him with us to the dog park on days like today when Teague subs."

My suspicions of Teague had eased some as time passed with no article appearing or other sign that he'd unearthed my secret. He still asked more questions than I liked, but he did it while building my shelves.

Still, I was *not* asking Teague O'Donnell for a key to his apartment.

Though if Clara chose to...

THE BOOKSHELVES WERE done, following the completion of the closet shelves.

Teague had finished packing up everything. All I had to do was wait a couple days for the last coat of paint to thoroughly dry before loading them.

That evening, he and I were in the office, toasting the completion.

I sat at the desk with champagne. He had his legs stretched out, the back of his neck propped on the back cushion of the loveseat, with a small bourbon.

The dogs were curled up together, each breath bringing them in contact with the sole of his propped-up shoe.

"I have an idea," I said.

"About?"

"Closets. The bedroom closets are way too small."

"That's how they built them back then."

"Yup. They also built them deep. And the closets to the two bedrooms are side by side. If the side wall was broken out, they could each have twice as much hanging space. And the shoe shelves wouldn't be disturbed."

"Huh. That might work. Want a bid?"

"Yup."

He gave me that half smile.

And another mystery was solved.

I'd been wrong that it was the smile of an interviewer. It was the smile of a detective.

The reason that half-smile bothered me was it indicated his brain was working away at some puzzle. Most of the time I'd seen it, he'd been looking at me.

Teague O'Donnell viewed me as a puzzle to solve.

That presented a problem, since I wanted to—needed to—remain unsolved.

"Call me Sheila M," he murmured.

"What?"

He rolled his head and looked at me from under his partly lowered lids. "I'm no English teacher, but I do like puzzles." I squelched a shiver at his echoing my thoughts. "I'll admit, this one, I had to write down. See it on paper. But then I figured out your game."

My heart squeezed, but my throat didn't. "My game?"

"First line of Moby Dick. *Call me Ishmael.* Happens to be an anagram for *Call me Sheila M.* No wonder you say it all the time. More English teacher humor."

I breathed.

✧ ✧ ✧ ✧

SOMEDAY I'LL TELL you the whole truth of how I came to Kentucky.

At least mostly, like Mark Twain did.

For now, I'll leave it that I moved to Kentucky.

Met the love of my life. Gracie the collie.

Found my spiritual home. The Torrid Avenue Dog Park.

And figured prominently—though the public doesn't know it—in the solution of a murder that baffled local law enforcement. (Is anyone other than law enforcement ever *baffled?*)

Oh, wait—there's one thing I'm not going to be truthful about. My well-known author name. (I'm being modest—my author name's famous.)

You'd know it. You'd tell your friends. And you might stop buying the books with that name on them. I couldn't do that to Aunt Kit. After all, she has an Outer Banks lifestyle to support.

Since I have a Haines Tavern, Kentucky, lifestyle to support, I'd be okay.

But I might need to get a job to feed Gracie's treat habit. And then I couldn't take her to the Torrid Avenue Dog Park as much.

The End

For announcements about upcoming books, as well as other titles and news, join Patricia McLinn's ReadHeads and receive her twice-monthly free newsletter.

patriciamclinn.com/readers-list

You can buy this book and all my others, including print editions and audiobooks, from my online store. I've added direct-to-you buying options to better control how my books reach you, while having lots more elbow room to give you special bundles, early offers, and exclusive bonuses.

Patricia's Bookstore

shop.patriciamclinn.com

Thank you for reading Sheila's latest adventure!

Sheila still has secrets to keep, but things are rolling along nicely in her new Kentucky home. That includes relaxing yoga classes with Clara at the Beguiling Way studio — until someone murders an instructor. Law enforcement says the killer was a passing-through stranger now long gone. Sheila and Clara have their doubts, and Teague has his own suspicions.

Death on Beguiling Way

Sheila, Clara, Teague, and friends ask if you'll help spread the word about them and the Secret Sleuth series. You have the power to do that in two quick ways:

Recommend the book and the series to your friends and/or the whole wide world on social media. Shouting from rooftops is particu-larly appreciated.

Review the book. Take a few minutes to write an honest review and it can make a huge difference. As you likely know, it's the single best way for your fellow readers to find books they'll enjoy, too.

To me—as an author and a reader—the goal is always to find a good author-reader match. By sharing your reading experience through recommendations and reviews, you become a vital matchmaker. ☺

Other Secret Sleuth cozy mysteries

DEATH ON THE DIVERSION

Final resting place? Deck chair.

DEATH ON BEGUILING WAY

Sheila untangles the untimely demise of a yoga instructor.

DEATH ON COVERT CIRCLE

A reviled supermarket CEO meets his expiration date.

DEATH ON SHADY BRIDGE

A cold case heats up.

DEATH ON CARRION LANE

Murder crashes Clara's high school reunion.

DEATH ON ZIGZAG TRAIL

Love and death decisions.

DEATH ON PUZZLE PLACE

Season's greetings: Whodunit?

"Move over Agatha Christie, there's a new sleuth in town. Patricia McLinn has created a fabulous new murder mystery series with … wonderful characters, both human and canine, [and] an interesting backdrop. I highly recommend." —*5-star review*

Caught Dead in Wyoming mysteries

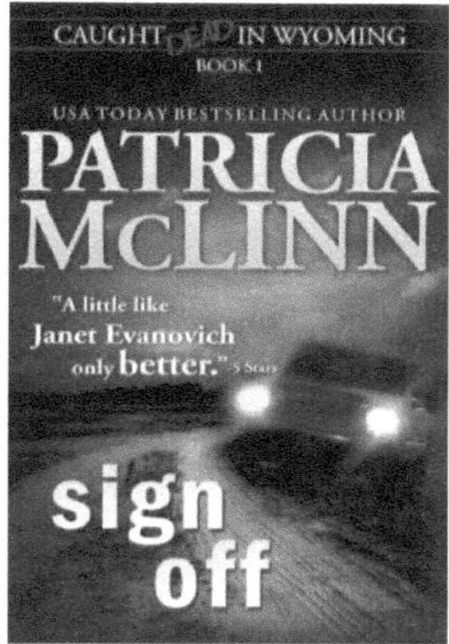

SIGN OFF

Divorce a husband, lose a career … grapple with a murder.

LEFT HANGING

Trampled by bulls—an accident? Elizabeth, Mike and friends must dig into the world of rodeo.

SHOOT FIRST

For Elizabeth, death hits close to home. She and friends delve into old Wyoming treasures and secrets to save lives.

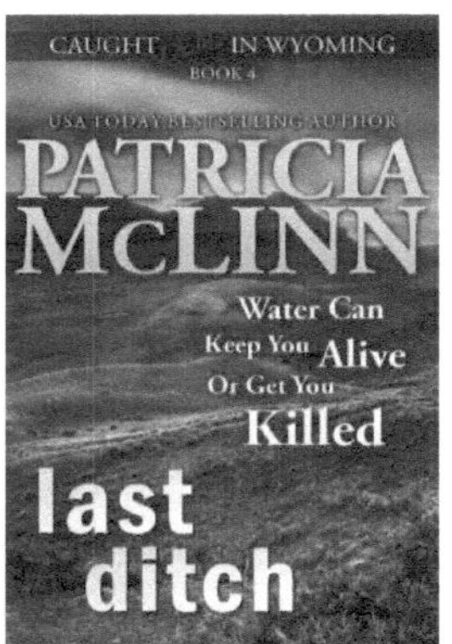

LAST DITCH

Elizabeth and Mike search after a man in a wheelchair goes missing in dangerous, desolate country.

LOOK LIVE

Elizabeth and friends take on misleading murder with help—and hindrance—from intriguing out-of-towners.

BACK STORY

Murder never dies, but comes back to threaten Elizabeth, her friends and KWMT colleagues.

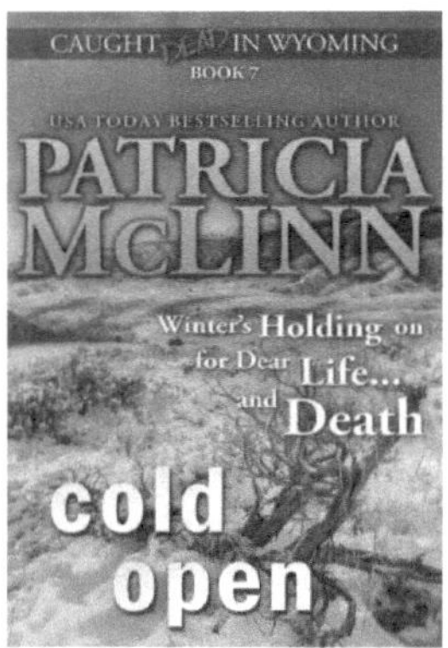

COLD OPEN

Elizabeth's looking for a place of her own becomes an open house for murder.

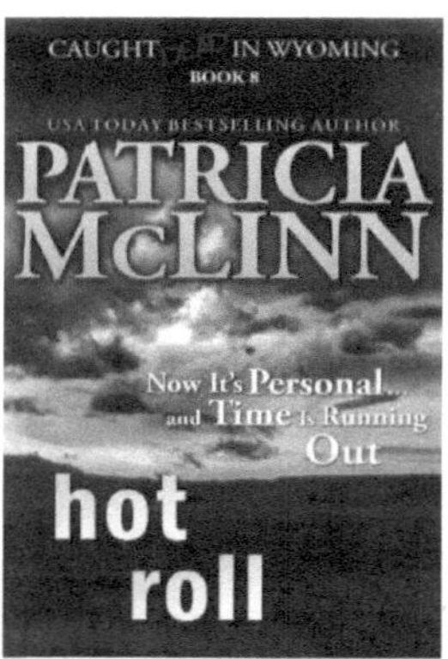

HOT ROLL

One of their own becomes a target—and time is running out.

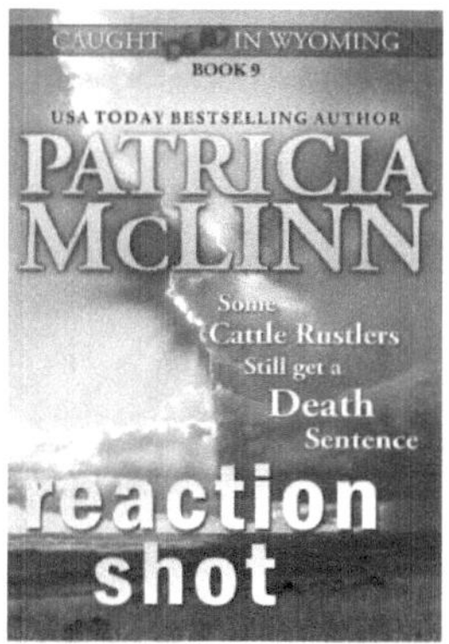

REACTION SHOT

Some cattle rustlers still get a death sentence.

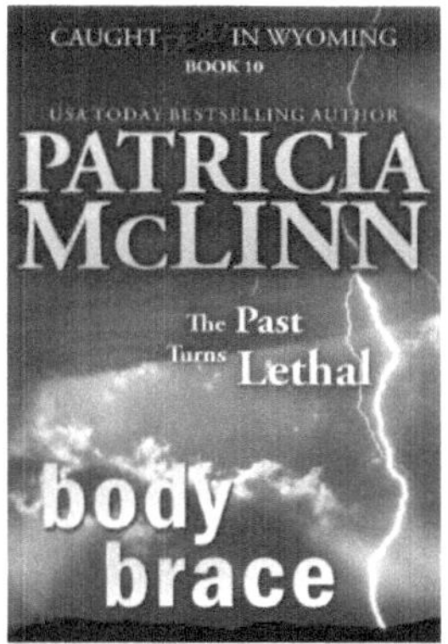

BODY BRACE

Everything can change … except murder.

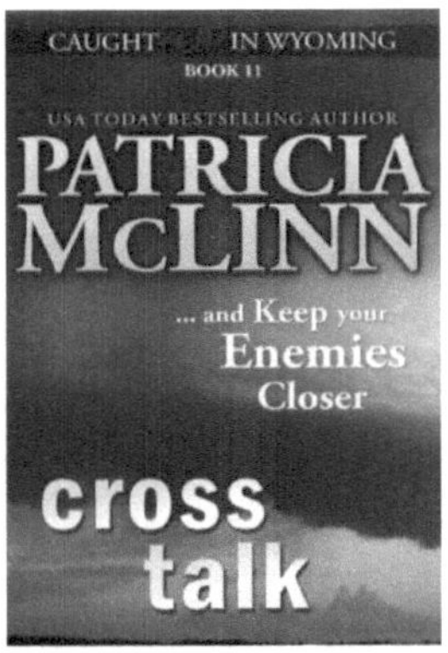

CROSS TALK

Prime suspect: the most annoying man in Sherman.

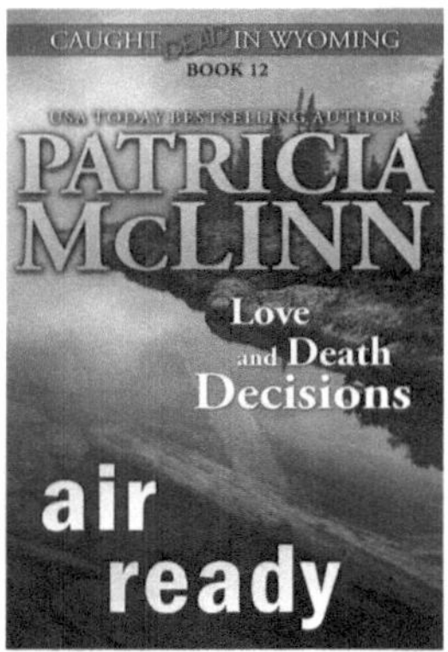

AIR READY

Love and death decisions.

HOLIDAY BULLETS

A Christmas wish with Elizabeth's name on it.

CUE UP

On the trail of murder.

Mystery With Romance

The Innocence Series

PROOF OF INNOCENCE

She's a prosecutor chasing demons. He's wrestling them. Will they find proof of innocence?

PRICE OF INNOCENCE

She runs a foundation dedicated to forgiveness. He runs down criminals. If they don't work together, people will die.

PREMISE OF INNOCENCE

The last woman Detective Landis is prepared to see is the one
he must save.

"Evocative description, vivid characterization, and lots of twists and
turns." —*5-star review*

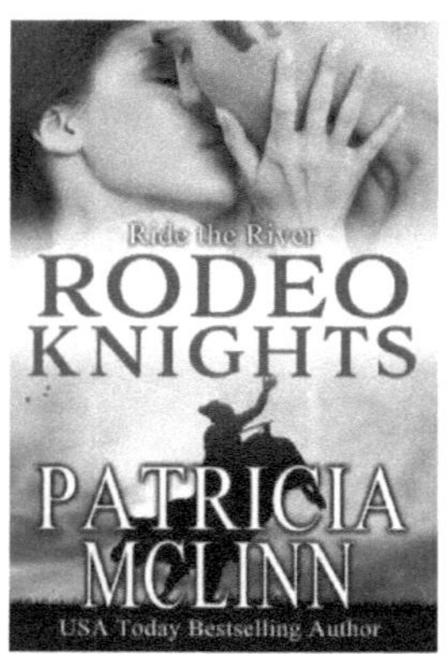

RIDE THE RIVER: RODEO KNIGHTS

Her rodeo cowboy ex is back … as her prime suspect.

Explore a complete list of all Patricia's books
patriciamclinn.com/patricias-books
Or get a printable booklist
patriciamclinn.com/patricias-books/printable-booklist

Patricia's Bookstore (buy online directly from
Patricia) shop.patriciamclinn.com

About the Author

Patricia McLinn is the USA Today bestselling author of more than 60 published novels cited by readers and reviewers for wit and vivid characterization. Her books include mysteries, romantic suspense, contemporary romance, historical romance and women's fiction. They have topped bestseller lists and won numerous awards.

She has spoken about writing from London to Melbourne, Australia, to Washington, D.C., including being a guest speaker at the Smithsonian.

McLinn spent more than 20 years as an editor at The Washington Post after stints as a sports writer (Rockford, Ill.) and assistant sports editor (Charlotte, N.C.). She received BA and MSJ degrees from Northwestern University.

Now living in Kentucky, McLinn loves to hear from readers through her website and social media.

Visit with Patricia:

Website: patriciamclinn.com

Facebook: facebook.com/PatriciaMcLinn

Pinterest: pinterest.com/patriciamclinn

Instagram: instagram.com/patriciamclinnauthor